Dream House

Justa Carpenter
www.justa-carpenter.com

Dream House

Copyright © 2012 by Justa Carpenter

Published by:
Healthy Life Press – 2603 Drake Drive – Orlando, FL 32810
www.healthylifepress.com
Printed in the United States of America

COVER AND INTERNAL ILLUSTRATIONS by Nikko Ellis Malerba
COVER DESIGN by Bill Wolff

Library of Congress Cataloging-in-Publication Data
Carpenter, Justa
Dream House

ISBN 978-1-939267-14-6

1. Christian Fiction; 2. Christian Living; 3. Adversity

HEALTHY LIFE PRESS was founded with a primary goal of helping previously unpublished authors get their works to market, and to reissue worthy, previously published works that were no longer available. Our mission is to help people toward optimal vitality by providing resources promoting physical, emotional, spiritual, and relational health as viewed from a Christian perspective. We see health as a verb, and achieving optimal health as a process – a crucial process for followers of Christ if we are to love the Lord with all our heart, soul, mind, AND strength, and our neighbors as ourselves – for as long as He leaves us here. We are a collaborative and cooperative small Christian publisher. For information about publishing with us, e-mail us at: healthylifepress@aol.com. To view our current resources, visit: www.healthylifepress.com.

Dedication

To the Divine Architect and Master Builder of all that is created and to His Project Manager who is faithful to complete every work He begins.

And to my wife, who patiently endures the mess I make whenever I try to help.

CONTENTS

PUBLISHER'S INTRODUCTION

THIS BOOK IS NOT A BIBLICAL COMMENTARY or theological treatise of any sort. It's just a story. And it's far more than just another good story.

Dream House was birthed after its author endured a severe trial that devastated his company and tested his trust in God's loving hand on his life. We had the pleasure of acting as a story-midwife in this case.

As Justa Carpenter was driving in his car one day, trying to figure out how to inform his family and crew that their funding had evaporated due to bank failure, and there was no more work, his thoughts were saturated with images of being on a journey through a jungle, which brought him to a mansion that was under construction. Looking bankruptcy in the face, he was reminded of the biblical promise that, "…He who has begun a good work in you will be faithful to complete it."

The author pulled to the roadside and recorded his thoughts. Then, after returning to his office, he wrote it down, so he would never forget it, and now you are unlikely to forget it, yourself.

I love this book! Not only because I know the author but because I know the author's Author, and I'm confident that this book will give you a new view of what it means to be His workmanship.

David B. Biebel, Publisher – Healthy Life Press

The Contract

ARCHITECT: GOD

BUILDER: JESUS CHRIST

PROJECT MANAGER: HOLY SPIRIT

OWNER: JUSTA CARPENTER

PROJECT NAME: DREAM HOUSE

PROJECT LOCATION: HEART

SCOPE OF WORK: JOHN 14:1-3; PHILIPPIANS 1:6

CONTRACT SUM: WHATEVER IT COSTS

COMPLETION DATE: WHEN IT'S DONE

PAYMENT SCHEDULE: PREPAID IN FULL

PLANS & SPECIFICATIONS: BY THE BOOK

SPECIAL TERMS: NO TURNING BACK

NO SUGGESTIONS

DON'T HELP

ACCEPTED BY: *Justa Carpenter*

CHAPTER 1
THE CONTRACT

THIS IS A STORY ABOUT A BUILDER who was a sincere follower of Jesus Christ. He was a successful builder and was very prosperous, building many homes each year.

Often at dawn, before he went to work, he would go to a secret place in the woods behind his house to meditate and pray and seek God's wisdom.

One day, as he was praying, he gave the Lord permission to do whatever He had to, to make his life count. He knew he was a child of God, but he often felt frustrated and unfruitful and afraid that somehow he was missing the best plan God had for him.

"Lord," he began, "I've had enough of me. I always seem to do what I don't want to do. I'm often stressed, I worry a lot and sometimes I take it out on others – especially those closest to me. What I am seems to be the opposite of who I want to be, and the very thing I don't want to do is what I often end up doing. Each time I try to give You control, something stronger than me takes it back and I end up worse than before."

There was something – a "presence" in his life that lurked in the shadows of his heart. It was difficult to define. At times, it was like a chameleon, blending in so perfectly that nobody could detect its presence. At other times it was agonizingly vile, blatantly self-serving, and it burst out when he least expected it. It was stronger than him and he knew he couldn't change who he was unless God intervened and did the changing.

As he wrestled that day with the unseen force, one that always seemed to dominate, he uttered a simple yet powerful prayer that unleashed an explosion of fury as two opposing forces went to war.

"Lord, please change me. Make my life count, whatever it costs," he said.

It was a rather peaceful morning on the day that he prayed his prayer. Sunbeams of light were streaking into the forest where he sat on an old birch log watching two deer grazing around a beaver pond below him. It was a special place. Off in the distance, a partridge was drumming for his mate and blue jays were just starting up their early morning banter. Squirrels played in the leaves and chased each other up and down the trees. It was a perfect morning to pray a perfect prayer. The man had offered an honest petition and in his heart he felt peaceful and right about it. It was a good start for the day with the Lord. He went off to work with a calmness about him that he hadn't felt in a while. He believed that he had prayed an acceptable prayer. What he didn't know was that it was about to be answered!

It was midmorning, just after his coffee break with the crew when everything came crashing down around him. It struck like a tornado from nowhere, leaving a path of devastation that his business would never recover from. His life would never be the same after that day. He left for work a prosperous and peaceful man, but by the time he returned home that night, he was financially devastated and deeply troubled – all in one day. It was hardly the result he had expected from such a fine prayer.

For years a battle raged between two forces within him. He was beaten down and pulverized by wave after wave of overwhelming predicaments that brought chaos and calamity; problems and trials he could not escape. What was once a paradise of fulfilled dreams and achievements had now become a battlefield of failure, bitter pain, and confusion.

It seemed like only yesterday, when there were challenges to overcome, and dreams to fulfill. Now everything was different. He felt humiliated as severe financial reversals plunged him toward inevitable bankruptcy. Icy realizations of impending failure sent shivers of weakness through his knees and joints. He wondered how he would explain to his family that they would soon lose their home and all their possessions.

Loneliness clung to him like wet clothes. He felt forgotten and abandoned by God. Even his closest friends, who were hurt by his demise, seemed secretly glad. Taking advantage of his wounded countenance and fearing for their own future, some falsely accused him and questioned the integrity of his faith.

How all these things happened didn't really matter to the man, but why they were allowed meant everything. Although he never questioned the basis of his faith, he did question God and spent countless agonizing hours searching for hidden and unconfessed sin. He even wondered about presumptuous offenses against God that he may have unknowingly committed.

He often considered the accusations of his friends, playing them over and over in his mind. He longed to just talk with them, but instead, he received long wordy letters and phone calls punctuated with anger, offering no hope of resolution. He could feel their pointing fingers in his face, blaming him for all their problems . . . and he believed some of it.

Day after day, his efforts to find solutions only made things worse. He felt like he had fallen into a hole that just kept getting bigger and deeper; a hole whose sides were too steep and slippery to climb out of. But it was a hole of his own digging and he knew it. Nightmares and huge anxieties robbed him of rest because he just couldn't stop blaming himself and thinking about it.

As the intensity of his problems continued to increase, his love for God turned to dread. Each morning and evening, he offered petitions for deliverance to the God he used to know. He confessed every sin he could call to mind and just to be thorough, he added a few extras. He claimed every promise he could find. He even tried to relinquish his fears as best he could, mentally placing them at the foot of the Cross like he had always been taught.

In spite of all his problems with lawyers, clients, employees, his own pastor and Christian brothers, however, he continued to be faithful to his church though he honestly wished he could sprout wings and fly away from it as far as he could get.

Finally, after several years, he stopped praying. He could only wait and hope . . . and be silent. He hurt like he had never hurt . . . and he despised himself more than ever in his life. He also despised his stupid sounding feeble prayers. They seemed forced and pointless, self-absorbed and pitiful. He hadn't given up praying. He just didn't know how to pray anymore.

At times, God seemed far away and unavailable. At other times, He seemed close but inaccessible, but no matter where God was, His response was always the same. There was just silence.

He wondered what had happened. God used to be his best friend. It was the joy in that relationship that had given him courage to dare against his inabilities. It had given him boldness to try new challenges – the kind that would stretch his faith and enable him to stretch even more. God had always honored such faith and prospered him. He always believed and he thrived by putting one foot in front of the other in faith, believing that God would establish his steps. He was a Jacob, in the sense that he wrestled in prayer for the blessing . . . but he was also a Jabez, who prayed simply and honestly just as if he was talking to his own father.

Now, it seemed like God had turned on him. To the man, God had become a harsh taskmaster, crushing him with impossible burdens and then judging him for his inability to bear them. He didn't know why. He wished that he did. Indeed, the man was crushed, for time had taken its toll. He could not imagine ever laughing again, for his eyes had lost the energy of life and his countenance diminished any evidence of hope. He finally gave up and just assumed the worst.

When we are attacked by the evil one, we know how to defend ourselves by faith, for God is greater, he reasoned. *When we are attacked by our neighbors for our faith, it isn't pleasant, but we rejoice in a way and are comforted, because we know it's Christ and the message of the Cross that they hate.* In hopeful reflection he continued, *When unjust accusations come upon us from our enemies or friends, He is our advocate to defend us, even when we're guilty.*

But then he just sat in silence. Years had passed and nothing had changed. A spiritual heaviness had landed on him as he asked himself the question he feared the most. *But, what does one do when he is convinced that the source of his problems is God? Where does one go for help? Who will deliver him then?*

With no strength left to fight, he gave up trying to defend himself and just agreed with everyone. *Maybe then, God will have mercy,* he rationalized.

It had been suggested by some friends and his pastor

that the reason he had so many problems was because he had been a cold-hearted, calculating, unfeeling, and worldly man, consumed only with himself. But inside, he hung on, knowing that he loved God and loved them deeply, too. At times, it angered him because they never talked to him about these things. They just talked with each other. Once, he was at a church retreat at a campground beside a beautiful lake in northern Vermont. He had attended with his wife; hoping to be encouraged, strengthened, and refreshed by being with his spiritual brothers and sisters. The first night as they both walked together in the pitch dark to the community bathhouse, a couple in front of them were talking about them; not knowing they were right behind them. They said very hurtful things, the kinds of things that pierce the heart and reveal secret feelings that were unknown. This couple worked for them and they always smiled when they were together. It was just another devastating moment, and they wanted to pack up their tent and go home. But they knew that if they did, then everyone would want to know why. So they stayed and stuck it out, wondering who else felt this way about them. It was unnerving. Instead of going home encouraged and strengthened, they went home with tears. He realized that the others had problems, too, and understood their fears. But he just wished they would try to understand his.

Vindication became his obsession, and these dark feelings surprised him . . . even scared him. Somewhere out of an unknown dungeon, in the shadows of morbid preoccupation, he more than compensated for their gossip with his own retaliations. He had never felt these feelings before. They surprised him and worried him a little. It bothered him that it felt good to strike back. These people were his friends, yet something in him had cracked and he couldn't control it. He had become very angry. He was bitter and cynical toward their worldliness, too. But what scared him the most was the creativity of his own attempts to cast aspersions on the reputation of others who had hurt him. He felt like he was in a cage of bitterness that prevented forgiving them and, from which he could only focus on getting even.

He despised the halo they wore in public. He hated the way they portrayed themselves as the victims and himself as the cause of all their financial woes. In sharing times, it seemed like many prayers were offered to God on their behalf, but none were offered for him. But then again, he was "The Businessman." He was the "rich man" in the Bible that even the apostles wished destruction upon. He got it loud and clear from everyone, including the pulpit. He had the bull's-eye on his back and a scarlet letter on his chest. He was a perpetual suspect for every hidden motive, every darkened agenda, every dastardly deed, and the cause of all the world's problems.

Such dark thinking felt good in a way, but he also felt deep shame at the same time. The net result was that he felt like a dirt pile on a very un-merry-go-round. He despised his "friends" for what they assumed and said about him, yet he also hated himself for despising them and wishing them ill. "No doubt, the Taskmaster will punish me for that, too," he muttered cynically. All the inner turmoil only made him feel worse, not better. So in the end, he wondered, *Perhaps they are right, after all. Maybe I really am that bad.*

This inner confusion hindered his human relationships, but it also affected his relationship with God. He used to approach the Throne of Grace with boldness. Now, he was terrified of God. He used to pray for hours. Now his praying was reduced to broken sentences and wishful longings, like meaningless gibberish. But it didn't matter. They just bounced back at him like a rubber ball off an iron ceiling, anyway. *What's the use in trying?* he wondered. He didn't know what to pray for, who to pray for, or even how to pray any longer. His anger with his friends had either subsided or submerged; he didn't know. But it had driven unwanted wedges between them – wedges of distrust that would take a miracle to dislodge. The loneliness and emptiness were taking their toll, and exhaustion left him tired of everything. He didn't even know how to feel tired. He didn't know to feel or think anything most of the time. Everything just seemed to go round and round, like a cyclone of mixed up feelings.

Maybe I've been fooling myself and I'm not even a Christian at all, he considered. *That would explain a lot about God's silence. But, if I'm not a child of God, then who is?* he wondered. *I understand about atonement and justification and I believe it. I understand the gift of God's grace and I stand there. I haven't moved. I know it's not about me. It's all about*

Christ and what He did on my behalf.

Such thoughts helped temporarily, but all too quickly the darkness turned to pitch-black and his depression turned to despair. He had never experienced such a terrifying sense of hopelessness in all his life. He had never thought he could go this low. Now, something had its grip on him and it was pulling him down. It kept telling him that he was evil; too evil to be saved. And when he listened, the cell he was in seemed locked and absolutely inescapable.

Yet even in that darkness, he heard a whisper: *Hang on. Hold fast.*

That voice reminded him that since he was a young child he had loved God.

But, did you really? another voice replied.

Remember the day you received Jesus Christ into your life at a Good News club? came the whisper.

But, did I really? he asked himself, this time. *Could an eight-year-old child really understand the gospel?* he sighed.

Even after all the years, vivid memories remained of what had happened that day. As Mrs. Cone, the Bible teacher, presented the gospel that afternoon on an old-fashioned flannel graph, he was sitting on her carpeted floor and watching her talk while she moved all the little felt people around. All of a sudden he realized that he was the sinner that was kneeling at the foot of the cross, the one she said was in desperate need of God's forgiveness. Even at age eight, he had "felt" the guilt and dirty feeling inside his heart and the sudden cleansing and freedom of forgiveness that came as he trusted Jesus to wash his soul clean and declare him blameless forever.

He even told his mom and grandmother about it and got baptized in front of the whole church a few years later.

During his runny nose, pimple and blunder years, he had been very active in his church, helping out wherever he was useful. He cared deeply for every member of the church, young and old. He had a deep affection for the old folks, like Pearly and Aletti, Margaret, Louise, Evelyn, and Nettie. There was something about their faith that he was very secure with. Even though their lives had been very hard, they seemed to "rest" in their faith and had great assurance of God's presence and promises. He liked being near them, and listening to them pray.

But . . . he wasn't a kid anymore, and as others accused him to his face he wondered, *Was it all to fulfill a need to feel significance and value? Was I doing it just to make myself feel better about myself? Was it simply to appease a guilty conscience; a self-righteous Novocain of sorts to hide the pain of truth . . . actually seeing myself for what I really was?*

As he stood between the flame of God's holiness and felt the chill of his own shame, he broke into a cold sweat. *If God is against me, then what do I have to live for?* he feared. Again, he accused himself . . . and again . . . he believed it. Every time . . . he believed it. The cage still seemed to imprison him, no matter what else might be true.

He was convinced there were hidden sins lurking in his heart; most likely of the presumptuous kind. They were the sins that God must be angry about. Even more, he began to think that it wasn't a matter of this sin or that sin which offended God, but simply his state of being. It wasn't so much about who he was before God but "what" he was.

He began to negotiate with God, accusing himself of idol worship and worldliness. He got rid of anything that he liked or had pleasure doing, fearing that he might love them more than he loved God. This took some time to do, for he was deep into some hobbies. He was convinced that he had fallen in love with the very blessings God had bestowed upon him. So he began despising them, too.

I will get rid of all of them, he thought. *Maybe then God will hear.*

In the courtroom of his mind, he declared himself "Guilty on all counts," and his spirit crumbled from his own indictment. How could he stand before such an awesome and holy God when he couldn't even stand before himself?

Has God withdrawn His Holy Spirit without my knowing, as he did with Saul and Samson? he feared. *Have I committed the unpardonable sin?*

He would not admit to that, yet he continued to whip and beat himself up hoping that his self-inflicted misery might evoke mercy, or his penitential actions might merit the grace that seemed to have been withdrawn and replaced by a voice that drove an iron stake into solid granite and shackled him to it, demanding his submission, and proclaiming, "I have you now. Your soul is mine, and there is nothing you can do about it, except DIE."

Yet he wrestled and clung and fought and hung on as his faith hovered in near ruin. And, somewhere, in pitch darkness, above the voice of relentless self-accusation, a compelling thought replied with firm assurance, "No . . . No . . . NO!" It was the loudest "inner whisper" he'd heard in a long time, and he could clearly hear its message, even above the roar of battle that was raging on the surface. "No, my son, you belong to ME."

He found comfort in the childhood promises he had memorized. He still believed them . . . he knew he did. There was still something solid there. It was deep down and planted well beneath his feet and had no intention of moving. Shifting sand never would have lasted this long.

Still, the futility of the struggle had ground down his ability to care about anything anymore. He didn't care about anger, he didn't care about love. He didn't care about living, nor did he care about dying. Tomorrow, he would put his house in order, what was left of it, and give up. So, even though he still barely clung to his faith, like the Old Testament character, Job, he finally cursed the day of his birth and he began to long for death as a way to escape the misery that had come upon him. The thought of death didn't bother him at all. It was a positive thought, a solution worth considering. Each day, it became increasingly desirable. He had long forgotten his casual prayer, "Lord, make my *life* count . . . whatever it costs." Now, it seemed, even his death would count for nothing.

That prayer had brought on such calamity and inner pain. It had cost him everything he thought he held dear. Yes, he could remember how, long ago, he had led the congregation in praise and singing. He had shared about the blessed hope within him with so many. Now, while others around him were lifting their hands and voices to God and growing by leaps and bounds and experiencing inner healing and testifying about answered prayers, he couldn't even lift his eyes off the floor.

Then, after many months of this inner turmoil, he re-membered that secret place in the woods and went back and sat there, not to contemplate or meditate, or to offer a litany of pious prayers. He returned there, just to sit. And after he had sat there in silence for a long time, fi-nally, almost whispering, he offered the only prayer he had left. Time had changed not only him but it had changed the way he approached God. He had no strength or resource left of his own as he uttered a simple prayer, this time from a pulverized spirit.

"Where are You?"

As a gentle breeze mingled with the warm summer sun, and leaves rustled in a pleasant monotone, the ex-hausted man fell into a deep sleep on a bed of soft green moss. It was there, in that secret place, that God replied, not with words, but with a dream that would change the man forever.

CHAPTER 2
INTO THE JUNGLE

H E FOUND HIMSELF STANDING IN A JUNGLE, far from order and civilization. It was an eerie place; a land of darkness and mystery. There was nothing about this jungle that resembled anything he came from. It was just the opposite. He had grown up surrounded by pastoral landscapes of Vermont hillsides. They had a way of saying, "Sit down and stay awhile." But instead of rolling meadows and open spaces, brooks and beautiful sunsets on distant Green Mountains, this jungle had a sinister, almost claustrophobic "Get me out of here" feeling. At first glance the jungle enticed the man's curiosity because it was so different from what he was accustomed to. Part of him wanted to just charge right into it, but his survival instincts restrained the childish impulse within him to explore. He needed to take his time to try and sort this out. He was no stranger to big swamps, but it was a bit too soon to just plunge into it.

Which way should I go?

Since he was six years old, when his father had begun taking him hunting, he had encountered many swamps while exploring the Northeast woods. But he had never seen one like this. Usually, he entered them slowly and very carefully, but even in spite of that, he seemed to always get cross-threaded to the point where he would have to navigate his way out by retracing his steps. Somehow, he never came out the same way he went in and there were even times when he emerged many miles from where he had started.

However, he was just beamed into this one, and it was different from any swamp he had ever encountered. Just the magnitude of it was stunning. Plus, he was already deep into it. There was no way to backtrack his way out because he didn't know how he had gotten there to begin with. Not only that, it was enclosed by a thick crown of leaves that prevented him from seeing very far in any direction. There was no sun available for his shoulder to align with or even a distant landmark to stay focused on. So he just stood there for awhile gazing at a network of trees, undergrowth, and shadows while he thought about what to do.

All around him was a wandering mist, slimy pits, and some rather tall, scary-looking grasses – the kind that wildcats, snakes, and gators lurk in. There weren't many options either. Although his first glance perceived only chaos, the man began to notice that there was, indeed, a certain consistency to the jungle. In a symbolic way, he had been in another jungle just like it. Except for the rolling Vermont landscape, his own world wasn't all that different from this one.

In this jungle, everything was either proactive or reactive. There was nothing that did nothing and so it was where he came from. He had felt it more than ever, especially recently. If he wasn't working hard at earning money for his family, he was doing everything he could to keep from spending it. It barely came in through a door only to fly out a window before he could get his hands on it. When he wasn't busy looking for his next job, he was trying to finish the one he was on. Nothing was working out. It wasn't unusual for him to bid low just to get jobs in order to keep his crew employed only to have everything go wrong and end up wishing he never got it in the first place.

As he studied the jungle, he noticed that most things were either growing or decomposing. Some things seemed to be growing and decomposing at the same time. It wasn't easy to distinguish between that which was beginning to live and that which had begun to die.

As far as he could tell, this jungle wasn't symbolic. It was the real deal and he was in it. He closed his eyes and opened them several times just to be sure. It was still there every time he looked and he knew that he had to deal with it. In order to do so, he had to get serious about moving on. So he began to take stock of his surroundings and develop a navigation plan. He wasn't taking one step without first developing a strategy. If he left the spot he was standing on, he wanted to be certain that he could find his way back to it if he needed to. Swamps have a way of just sucking you in and when you turn around to retrace your steps, the place you just stepped on has sunk into the mire, eliminating the option of going back the same way you came. He knew that exercise all too well.

In this jungle, everything thrived on the edges of shadow and light. Life and death were as interactive as the rain and sky was with the mist and the marsh. He preferred light and wasn't looking forward to spending a single night in the darkness, especially with no way of defending himself. The most light was right where he was standing and there was one thing that stood out that he didn't remember any other swamp having. This jungle or swamp, or whatever you choose to call this place he was standing in, was populated by an obvious presence.

The trees. All around him were enormous trees. They were taller and wider trees than he'd ever seen, even in pictures. They dwarfed everything underneath them, especially the man, whose microscopic presence made him feel very insignificant. *Who am I?* he wondered. *I feel like a tiny ant standing next to these trees.*

The trees were taller and wider than the biggest Redwood and they had an aged patina that would make the most ancient Sequoia seem like a mere adolescent. Their mystery rose out of a murky bog and intersected with a lofty purpose high above, where nobody could see.

As he studied their dominance and precision, he realized that they had been evenly spaced and were as true in vertical stature as a builder's plumb line. Each one had

25

to have been planted with precise calculation and purpose. *But by whom?* he wondered. *And when?*

Although each tree seemed to be by itself, no tree stood alone. Their canopies were all interconnected and they shared a network of influence over everything below. Their bark was especially intriguing. It had the appearance of oiled bronze and resembled something that had been hand-brushed and buffed by time, itself. They were as smooth and unblemished as a polished flagpole and their towering stem offered no way to climb.

Throughout the jungle, these monarchs ruled. There was no other way to explain them. Without uttering a single word, they spoke in unified voice, saying, "All Authority is mine over the sky above and everything on earth below." They offered no hint of democracy; only sovereign rule. The trees were the law. They ruled fearlessly, without regard for other opinions or philosophy. It was a place where consensus had no vote. They determined whether occupants in the jungle existed or didn't, simply by their presence.

But they were far from unfriendly. On the one hand, they seemed to enjoy concealing the mystery of their purpose, while at the same time they challenged their guests to search for it. The man wasn't afraid of them – well at least in most ways – and he felt a growing affection for them. Other than their pure size and strength, there was another attribute about the trees that made them unique to everything else in the jungle. In order to learn anything about them, the man could only look upward.

The trees were wrapped in mystery and the man wondered about it as he studied them. He asked himself the usual questions, *How did they get here? Who put them here? How long have they been here? What were they doing here?* But who could he ask? It was as if there was a spirit inviting him to search for the answer, yet he didn't know how or where to start looking.

The jungle knew the answer to the mystery of the trees, but it was not allowed to speak. It could only observe those who passed through and how they reacted to their presence. Throughout the ages, many travelers had tried to explain them in their own way. How else could they explain them? Was there another way to understand the trees besides trusting in their own understanding? The answer was right in plain sight, but it was too pure and too simple for many travelers to accept. No wisdom was required in order to explain their presence; neither was intellect required to find the path through the jungle. The message of the trees, when comprehended, either drew travelers toward them or it repelled them away. There were some who just tolerated the trees. But most travelers either loved the trees or they hated them. Those who loved them stayed near them and grew in their affection for the trees. Those who hated the trees just wanted them gone. They didn't care how. They just wanted them out of their way.

They wouldn't accept the notion that all of life in the jungle was held together by the network of trees, and without them, all life would cease to exist.

That indisputable fact didn't matter to those who hated the trees because they hated the authority that the trees held over them ... the authority of truth - immutable, unchangeable, eternal. They thought of the trees as a sort of bondage, because they preferred to create and combine their own individual versions of truth, as if truth were relative, and therefore open to discussion among those claiming to be pursing it. "We have studied the writings," they claimed - though most of the writings they had studied were not the foundational writings but the writings of interpreters of the original writings. "And we have concluded that truth is not something to be known, but something to be sought. So we are satisfied to remain seekers of truth." Being thus perpetually engaged in the process of learning, these "seekers of truth" never came to actually know and embrace the truth, and they all fell to their destruction, taking many others with them.

Over the millennia of time, the jungle had observed many groups of travelers come through. Many of them believed that any rational-thinking, open-minded person would agree that there are many paths through the jungle. The notion that there was only one safe path through was far too exclusive to be true. As a result of this presupposition, the most tolerant, and those who followed them, had all fallen into the pit.

If the jungle could offer only one audible comment for travelers to hear, it would be a heavy sigh and a long sad groan. It would groan in unison so loudly that the groans of the trees would drown out all other sounds,

The Blind Leading the Blind

even the sound of the traveler's screams when, just before they perished, they realized the folly of their thinking. But the jungle wasn't allowed to speak. It could only stand in full display without saying a word. The trees spoke loud enough. They were "The Word" without speaking a word.

It was always a happy day when a traveler came along and believed the message of the trees. Most of them usually came alone.

If the jungle could talk, it would share that the very swamp, itself, was fed by the tears of angels who wept as they observed many choose their own path to certain death, when right in front of them was the only means that provided safe passage. They often heard the question asked, "How could a loving God send good people to hell?" But, there in front of the jungle, stood the only safe passage; plain, simple, and true . . . and available to all. This forced the only reply that could be offered, "Why would good people choose to go there?"

It was a perpetual and painful display of folly, one that brought great sorrow to its observers. As soon as one group departed from the safety of the trees and went off on their own, they soon became disoriented and lost and imperiled in the chaotic and predatory nature of the jungle. None were spared. They all perished because there was no other path. Then, in what seemed like only minutes in the scale of time and eternity, another group would come along and do the same, thinking they could improve on means and methods used by the groups that had perished before them. In their collective minds, they were confident that "They wouldn't make the same mistakes. They would do it right." But they didn't do any better than the groups before them because the truth didn't change: There was only one safe path through the jungle – follow the trees.

To understand the message required no credential or diploma. It demanded no robe or collar to wear. It was available to everyone in equal measure, not just to the so-called noble, elite, educated, or wise. Even children could understand the message of the trees.

To those who were humble enough to accept it with the faith of a child, the answer to the mystery of the trees was obvious: "They were there. They had always been there, and they would always be there." In humility, each one accepted in their own heart this truth about the trees: **Before I was, they were. And long after I'm gone, they still will be.**

As the man rested for a moment, his mind began to open. He perceived that everything that lived, breathed, and existed in the jungle was granted its own existence by the trees. The trees were both judicial and relational. The trees spoke, and everything else complied.

By now, the man trusted the trees more than he trusted his own instincts. He much preferred leaning on them than leaning on his own strength and intuition to get through the jungle.

It was settled. The man wasn't going to change his mind. They weren't a truth or his truth. They were "The

Truth."

"Truth simply 'is'," he remembered his father telling him when he was a kid. "That which is not true 'is not' and whatever poses as something that is, but is not, is a lie. People lie when they want you to believe something that isn't." His father had taught him that, and had also told him that, "Someday every lie will be exposed for what it isn't, and the only thing left standing will be that which truly is. So search for that which you know is true and, when you find it, stand there. Pay no mind to the ear-ticklers." The man never forgot it, either. If only he had practiced it. Why did it always have to be so obvious in hindsight?

The man had arrived with exhausted resources, and any remaining self-reliance had vanished long ago. He also didn't need anyone to convince him that he needed help. He not only needed the trees; he wanted them. He believed that their presence was no accident. He feared them and loved them at the same time. He was glad they were there and he accepted the boldness of their statement.

"I AM," they chorused, with a thousand echoes. "Before the jungle was, I AM."

The man had developed a deep affection for the trees and he felt safe standing next to them. Under his feet, their exposed roots mingled with an endless vine, tangled somewhere between the surface and midair. The vine, with its thick hairy skin, threaded itself between the smooth barky roots, weaving a natural bridge over the murky bog below.

In other places, it hung loosely like a swinging rope, providing easy transportation from one tree to the next. Even though he left one tree and swung over to another one, something inside suggested to him that they weren't separate trees. They were all the same tree.

As time went by and he exposed his own presence with constant movement, the man became more aware of increasing sounds around him. The trees had preoccupied him and they had also concealed him, but now he had been detected and the growing intensity of sounds was beginning to make him feel a bit uneasy. At first there had been a peaceful silence as the concealed residents of the jungle sized up their new visitor. It made him feel safe and away from danger. But now, as each moment passed and the man's presence seemed less threatening, life in the jungle resumed with its ageless and aggressive resolve.

Soon, the air became thick with turbid repetitions of violent thrashing and morbid silence. There were no songbirds in the jungle; only predators. There was no singing or serenades. There were only sounds of the predators' roars and chilling screams of their victims. Then, as each roar echoed throughout the jungle, its victory chant would soon be cut short as the predator became the next victim to another and to another in an endless cycle of death and carnage. The jungle floor revealed what was truly there. It was crawling with life-taking-life. It was a place where survival staked its claim in the deepest flow of blood, and dominance built its kingdom on

The Trees Ruled the Jungle

the bones of its victims.

For a moment, as the man observed life's uncertainty played out beneath him, he recalled his own achievements and how hard he had worked to earn them. It seemed that he no sooner had them in his grasp than he, too, was stripped of them. He sighed heavily as he observed the futility of self-preservation played out in the muck below, realizing that his life was no different. He began to wonder what he'd gotten into.

The trees fascinated the man. He liked them. He was glad they were there. They provided a sense of protection and security. He shuddered to think about what it would be like to try and make it through the jungle without them.

The towering, branchless trunks had such smooth bark that no creature could use them for advantage. That made him feel safe. Not only that, they were much too broad in circumference to grip and because of their polished surface, they were impossible to climb. From the top, if they ever did get climbed, they were simply too high to pounce from. No creature could profit from the trees or manipulate them to fit their agenda.

Then there were the vines. Like the trees, they, too, offered no place for comfortable perch. While standing, one could only lean against one of them or use it to swing on. The vine was a useless place for predators to just hang onto because they would simply expose themselves in plain sight until too exhausted to keep their grip. He smiled as he imagined a dangerous "predator" passing by on a swinging vine, swiping at its next meal. It was a funny thought. He liked "funny." It helped him relax. He was starting to figure it out.

It was obvious to the man that all the predators were confined to the murky shadows of the jungle floor. Their only device was to deceive and camouflage, lurking in the shadows of undefined darkness, depending on their own skill, deception, and concealment. They were ineffective in the light and could be easily avoided when exposed. That explained why the trees and the vine and the roots were devoid of occupant. They served three different functions while working in unity to achieve one purpose. The man began to understand that they provided a true navigational path, a way to travel, and a safe place to stand. As long as he trusted all three, he was in a safe place; a place where nothing could pluck him off. The thought revived him and gave him hope. This was too coincidental to be a coincidence.

Can't stay here, he concluded optimistically. *Nuf pondering. Gotta get going, if I'm ever gonna get outta this place.*

His new perceptions and the challenge seemed therapeutic and gave the man something he hadn't had in a long time . . . hope, and something to overcome. He reached out and clung to the vine with both hands, balancing his tender feet on its ropelike threads. It was time to get moving, for he could barely keep his feet from slipping through the skinny network of roots and vine. His feet were beginning to hurt, and moving was his only remedy. The roots never allowed him to stand still for very long.

The pattern of undergrowth changed as he moved along. Much of the tall grasses and ferns were giving way to a friendlier-looking landscape. He could see a little further across the boggy floor and it didn't feel so closed in. In every direction, there were curious looking rusty flats surrounded by green slimy muck. In between, there were intermittent pods supported by the roots and the vine under a low ceiling of constantly-shifting fog.

As the man began to plot his course, he realized that his choices were limited if he was going to stay safe and dry. His options were very few. He could only transport himself by swinging from one pod to another, and the vine was the only means by which he could do it. Yet, as he swung from pod to pod, trying to find his bearings, a question began nagging him: *Where am I, and how did I get here?* He also added, cynically, *And it would be nice to know where I'm going!* Since the trees were positioned in rectangular quadrants, the man never really knew whether to go forward or back or to the right or to the left. In every direction, there was another tree that he could choose to safely swing to. It confused him, but he knew that he should just keep moving anyway.

Underneath his feet, through the roots and tangled vines, he could see the movement of floating slime and moss. On his right and left, throughout the bog, light brown flats of firm-looking soil continued to entice him with a tempting lure. *A different path through the jungle!* he thought. *There can't be only one path through the jungle, can there?* Hadn't he already determined that? But things had changed from before. Now there were a lot of things about the light brown flats that looked pretty good to him. Maybe the trees had brought him to solid ground and it was okay to let go now.

They sure look like a better place to stand, he reasoned.

These hardened roots are killing my feet! The smooth-looking flats were within jumping distance, yet the vine only hung suspended over each pod. The man knew he would have to let go of the vine in order to jump over to the flats. He also knew he wouldn't be able to reach the vine again, once he let go of it. The vine was elevated far above the jungle floor and there was no way to climb back onto the network of roots that stood so high above everything else.

Soft sand, and a place to lie down, he thought wistfully. *It looks so good; its got to be right. I'm sure it would be a much easier walk from there. Those flats practically touch each other, too. I won't even need the vine.*

The enticement of freedom from the roots and from the vine tempted him to think that he no longer needed the vine, so he decided to take a closer look. He leaned out almost horizontally, precariously hanging onto the end of it. He stretched his neck out as far as he could to get a closer look at the sandy-looking flat. By this time, his only connection to the pod was the tips of his toes. He had fully extended himself. Now, only a few feet away, he noticed something a little bit unusual about the flat. For a split second, the dimly lit jungle seemed to get brighter and the brown sand suddenly didn't look quite right. It seemed to heave and swell a bit.

Solid ground doesn't move, he thought. *Maybe it's just my imagination. It's been a long day*, he thought as he nervously squeezed the vine. *What else could it be?* Suddenly, something inside him screamed, *Watch out! QUICKSAND!*

It startled him and a sudden rush of fear made him lose his balance as he tried to scramble back to the security of the pod. He had extended himself too far, and his feet slipped off the roots, slamming into the vise-like jaws of the quicksand below, filling his trousers with its toxic ooze and giant leeches. He dangled precariously, trying to pull himself up, while all around him, he heard the thrashing of movement and splashes coming toward him as he hung, suspended half in and half out. He panicked, realizing that he was an easy grab for anything that was hunting for a meal.

His body felt heavier and his fingers strained with each attempt to pull himself free. Little by little, he inched his way up the vine until his feet finally came out. He managed to work the vine back and forth until he planted his feet back safely on the pod. His arms and upper body were exhausted and he was very glad he hadn't jumped. Suddenly he was thankful for the security of the roots, even though they hurt his feet. "Leeches" he muttered to himself, "I hate leeches. They only have one purpose, to suck blood." They reminded him of his own self-inflicted problems that had sucked the lifeblood out of his dreams back home. *I wonder how close those predators got to me?*

Clinging to the Vine

he thought as he rested and regained his strength. *That was too close.*

The flats of quicksand were cleverly disguised traps to even the most experienced traveler. As if designed by evil intellect, they thrived on trickery and shadows, inhaling every careless victim who didn't look closely before jumping. Their thick rusty scum lay in magnificent stagnant harbors of earth-colored ooze and grassy moss, posing as solid ground. Each seductive patchwork advertized its deceptive promise to any impulsive traveler who might be looking for reprieve from the slimy bog and uncomfortable roots, blistered hands, and the trees.

The man had seen through its trickery just in time, but he was stunned by how real it had looked when it was so obvious now.

Perhaps he just wanted to believe there was a more comfortable place to stand and easier way to travel. He didn't want to admit that it bothered him a little that the trees never changed and that he just wanted some variety in his life, not just the same old . . . same old, even if it really was his only hope of surviving in the jungle. He wondered how many others had preceded him on this same quest . . . but hadn't made it. They had followed the path for awhile, but for various reasons had decided they didn't want to follow it any longer. The quicksand had swallowed them up. He knew that the reason he was still alive was because of the perfect timing of that sudden glimpse of light that was permitted through the canopy above. It had revealed everything just in time. *Hardly co-*

incidental, he mused.

Catching his breath, the man thankfully clutched the vine with both hands, blisters and all. He shuddered at what might have been, had he let go of it. As he leaned with his back against the tree and looked skyward, he marveled with growing affection at the complexity and majesty of the trees, yet he also marveled at the simplicity of their purpose. He was relieved to know that he could depend on them to keep and preserve and deliver him to the other side. The vine was woven securely to the towering trees above, and he was thankful for their solid connection to each other.

Still shaken by his awareness of what had almost happened, and struggling to compose his thoughts, he became much more cautious and scrutinizing as he carefully inched his way through the bog. His fears kept him preoccupied with doubts and they constantly caused him to lose confidence in his own confidence. He didn't know where he was going. How could he? A question came to mind that was once asked by one of Jesus' disciples, "How can we know the way?" Thomas had asked. To which Jesus had responded, "I am the way, the truth, and the life." And then he remembered another saying of Jesus, "I am the vine, and you are the branches...."

Just cling to the vine. Whatever you do, don't let go, an inner voice reminded him. *The vine hasn't let you down yet.* Time passed with endless redundancy, as he left one pod and swung to the next, trying to find his way through. Nothing ever changed. Each pod was identical to the next, and he never knew if he should go frontward or backward or to the side. He suspected that he was going deeper into the jungle because whatever light there had been before was slowly diminishing. In its place, murky fog had begun settling onto the jungle floor, casting a musty spell throughout the dense underbrush. It hovered over the stagnant muck and even over the roots, making it difficult to distinguish between safe passage and unstable footing. He was running out of light, and a sense of lostness now pervaded everything. He was having trouble even seeing the next pod. Increasing panic compelled him to move quicker and quicker.

Phantom shadows began playing tricks on him, pretending to be formless monsters. The inner stress to find his way out only drove him faster and faster forward. He couldn't imagine going backward. It would soon be night. He had to continue on, quickly. For a moment, he gave up and sat down. *One wrong move and I'm dead!* he despaired. *I'm dead anyway. I'm never going to get out of here. How did I ever get into this mess? Where in the world am I?*

He had no idea how he had gotten there. He had no idea where he was, and he knew nothing about where he was going. He was just going . . . somewhere . . . or nowhere.

I've got to keep searching, he said to himself. There's got to be a way out. *Just keep moving and don't give up. You just gotta have faith.* He laughed bitterly at such a notion. *Faith in what? For what? Everyone says you just gotta have faith.* But the man knew how stupid that sounded and he thought, *What's the point of faith if it has no object or promises no hope?*

As he sat clinging to the vine, he felt like a shipwrecked seaman holding onto water-soaked debris wondering how long it would take for the sharks to come. His faith used to have purpose and direction, movement and zeal, dreams and achievements. Now, like the seaman, his faith was reduced to merely hanging on. The seaman had his plank. The man had his trees and his vine and the roots. The trees were always the same. They were strong and they never moved. They also supported the vine. The trees ruled over everything beneath them, yet the vine provided the only way to move through the jungle. The roots preserved his life by allowing him a safe place to stand, far above the dangers that lurked below. The three worked together in unison and were delivering the man through the jungle. He comforted himself with the fact that they had preserved him so far and because of that, he also believed that they would deliver him the rest of the way.

Dream House

CHAPTER 3
THE MONSTER

AS TIME WENT BY, THE MAN SENSED A NEW DANGER. It was predatory and it wanted him. It was close by and it made him forget that he was lost. Something was following him. He was sure of it. He couldn't see or hear it. He just sensed it was there and that it had but only one thing on its mind.

Perhaps it had sensed his vulnerability. In his mind, he imagined the ease of its movement while feeling the difficulty of his. It followed easily behind him, dancing from pod to pod as if playing games with him. It was evil and cunning, and it understood him. It was catlike and shrewd. It was merciless and patient. It slowly paced and watched him. It played with him, instilling terror, waiting to pounce when its surprise would be most "effective."

But it was more than catlike. Even cats had more powerful enemies. This "thing" was a monster; way bigger than any cat and its patience was no virtue. It was pure strategy.

A Terrifying Predator

To the man, it was the most powerful and fearless of all the predators in the jungle, and it could get him any time it wanted him. He was no match for it. It was at its best in the pitch black. He wasn't.

Every time the man tried to crawl an inch to get away, he would feel driven closer. No matter what he tried to do, he felt like he was merely doing it a favor. This thing was in it for sport. Killing him would be the easy part. What fun is that? It was much more entertaining to watch him squirm and try to escape.

The man was totally exposed. He couldn't climb the trees to get away and there was no place on the roots to hide. His convenient location would make his disposal especially easy, leaving nothing but a splat for future travelers to observe where the sum total of his meaningless life had once existed.

Fear and fatigue were settling in. So was a bit of exasperation. Once, in a moment of desperate courage, the man decided to just face the monster. Turning quickly to look behind him, he thought he saw a movement. It was a shadow without form that was every bit as confusing as the jungle around him, but he couldn't be sure if there was even anything there at all. At other times, it felt so close, he could smell either his own fear or his imminent death as it brushed by his cheeks in the dense fog.

By now, his hands hurt from holding so tightly to the vine, but he didn't dare let it go. It was his only hope. He couldn't let go . . . ever. Only the prospect of getting out of that jungle would convince him to ever let go again.

The encroaching mist now felt like a thick soupy current of slithering death. Each movement of his body sent new waves of undefined terror swirling around him, and it seemed to only add to the creature's advantage. The fog was so thick now, the man couldn't see anything.

His tortured mind was convinced that the evil thing could be slithering down the hairy vine, hovering just inches above his head, almost touching him with its icy breath. Then a new and more terrifying thought occurred to him,

Perhaps it will strike from below!

His fear went wild and his heart beat uncontrollably as he could only imagine that thing waiting for the right moment to explode upon him from out of the creepy sludge below. Yet, it was still just a feeling, and for each circumstance there was always an explanation rebuking his paranoia. *Am I going crazy?* he asked himself. *First, I think I hear things and now I'm convinced that something is following me, and I can't even see it.*

He didn't know how much longer he could distinguish between reality and that which didn't exist, and he doubted his ability to endure much longer. Finally, still clinging to the vine, he bowed his head, relinquishing his predicament to his Creator, and once again, he desperately asked for help. He had used up all his resources and was still hopelessly lost. His faith was running on fumes. It couldn't get much darker, and all his strength was gone.

As the jungle became black with the final passing of daylight, he was afraid to raise his head and even look above him. He dreaded the thought of being there all night.

"Darkness," he prayed with poetic simplicity. "The darkness of the jungle, the darkness of night, the darkness of not knowing; Lord, please send me Thy light."

As he finished praying, he looked up and saw a strange glow emanating through the tree tops, similar to the one that had revealed the quicksand. The fog had lifted briefly, revealing dry leaves and a small firm embankment directly in front of him.

The edge of the bog! he thought excitedly. *It's just one step away!*

It was so close, yet even then he didn't know whether or not to trust his own perception. Suddenly another glimpse of light revealed that solid ground was truly right in front of him. His doubts instantly vanished and he knew the vine had delivered him through the jungle. It was time to make his move. It was now or it would be never.

That thing, whatever it is, only works in darkness; maybe it won't follow me toward that light! he thought with revived hope.

Without hesitation, he bolted up the hill and with all his heart, strength, and soul, he thrust his body into a barrier of tangled briars, hoping to break through them. Branches and thorns shredded his clothes and tore into his skin but nothing would stop him from getting through. His legs and arms were bleeding and his muscles were burning and his lungs felt like they were about to explode as he scrambled upward toward the light. As

Into the Light

he approached the top of the hill, he jumped over a final windfall and in summersault fashion he hurled his body into a clearing, landing flat on his back. He laid there with his eyes closed. His heart was pounding and his lungs were gasping and wheezing for breath.

CHAPTER 4

THE MANSION

THE SOURCE OF LIGHT WAS COMING FROM A CLEARING at the top of a small hill in front of him. He had never been that frightened, even when he had taken a wrong turn in Harlem one night and ended up in a dead-end alley. He had been pretty scared then, but that paled in comparison to being hunted by this evil creature. *What was it? Did it follow me?* he couldn't help wondering. He knew this could be it. He had nothing left. *I just can't go any further. I'm done!*

At any second, he expected tons of beast and predator to lock its deadly jaws upon his exhausted body, and he accepted the possibility of a violent death. He was too tired to move and didn't even dare to open his eyes. He just hoped it would be quick.

Bruised and bleeding, he hadn't noticed the soft and plush green grass that he had landed on. His thoughts were only of surviving, and getting away from that "thing."

A long time passed before he began to hope that the danger was gone. He also noticed new sounds. They weren't the kind of spooky sounds he'd heard in the jungle. These were the sounds of songbirds.

"Songbirds?" he whispered as he slowly opened his eyes. "Here?"

As he lay there with outstretched and exhausted arms, he noticed that his landing spot was of unusually good choice. His hands, feeling the smooth silky blades of soft grass between each finger, gently stroked the ground back and forth. The velvety cushion beneath him helped support his aching muscles. It felt good and helped him to relax.

There was also something else he hadn't seen in a long time – daylight and crystal blue sky. He stood up on his shaking knees and brushed off the dirt and slime that had clung to him on his hasty flight to safety. He hadn't noticed that he had landed at the edge of a beautiful garden adorning the entrance to an impressive estate . . . until now. The man, having barely recovered from one episode, now looked around in startled disbelief.

"Now where am I?" he cried. "First the jungle, now this!" The confusion of startling contrasts bewildered him, and for a moment, he just stood there collecting his thoughts . . . and himself. He had been certain that he hadn't died, but maybe now he wasn't so sure. This was too surreal to be real. *But dead people don't have tired muscles, do they?* he wondered. *They also don't get hungry or bleed and gasp for breath, either!* His lungs still hurt. It's not like he worked out in a gym every day. He was an office guy and when he wasn't sitting behind a desk or at a computer designing homes, he was driving his car somewhere two hours away and going to meetings at night.

Well, he said to himself while nervously keeping one eye toward the edge of the jungle, *I may not know where I am, but one thing I do know: Nothing and I mean No THING can get me to go back in there.*

Through the garden landscape of mature oaks and willows, he could make out the silhouette of a huge mansion on the far end of an endless rolling lawn. There was a cobblestone path directly in front of him weaving its way through flowerbeds, overhanging fruit trees, and miniature waterfalls of crystal clear water. He was thirsty and drank from the fountain until he couldn't drink any more. Then he ate some nearby juicy pears and shiny red apples until he'd had his fill. Then he stood . . . and just looked. What else could he do but look?

Throughout the garden, tingling rays of sparkling light hung suspended in a cool misty fog and the songbirds were everywhere! It was a spectacular sight to the shaken and disheveled man, yet it was still a bit unsettling and difficult to comprehend. With his torn clothes and filthy appearance, he felt out of place, and worried that he would soon be discovered and told to leave. But where would he go? He knew where he wouldn't go.

As he walked along the stone path he paused to observe his new surroundings. The organized life and pat-

Wow!

tern of this magical sight followed all too quickly in frightful contrast to the darkness and confusion that had owned him in the jungle. He had just escaped a world where predators feed on predators only to be propelled into an opposite scenario; a garden of songbirds feeding their young in peace and safety right out in the open. *Even back home, where it was relatively safe for most birds, they still wouldn't expose their chicks for fear of crows and jays,* he thought. *But these little birds live with no fear of anything?* He realized that he hadn't heard the caw-caw of a single crow or tattle-tale screams of the thieving murderous blue jay; only the melody of songbirds. But then his thoughts were interrupted as the path led him around a pond and turned him into a long row of giant oaks on both sides of the path. At the other end was a structure that overwhelmed the man.

"Wow or double wow or whatever wow! How about awesome?" he whispered in a reverent tone. Right in front of him, now just a few hundred yards away, the mansion seemed perfectly placed like a bride on center stage. He couldn't help but feel strangely drawn to it. He didn't know why, but as fear gave way to curiosity, he boldly continued his approach. Pausing again for a moment on a footbridge spanning a small brook, he looked behind him and wondered if he would ever return. Even though it had been several hours since he had made his escape from the jungle, his heart was still pounding. His legs still quivered from his close encounter with that "thing," and he didn't know if his heart was pounding from his escape or if it was pounding because of what was standing right there in front of him.

Return? he wondered. *Return where?*

His mind couldn't let go of the events that had brought him there. The quiet and serene flow of the brook helped to calm his jittery nerves. He decided to leave the path for a moment and just walk in the manicured grass alongside the brook as it meandered toward the mansion. It felt soft on his feet and his feet desperately needed to feel something soft. All the while he walked along the edge of the brook, he never lost sight of the mansion.

As each moment passed and each step brought him closer to it, the flowing architecture and the fine details of its magnificent form began to relieve his mind with newer and less anxious thoughts. Even from a hundred yards, he could already discern some incredible details.

He was just a carpenter, but he had always dreamed of building a mansion of his own. He knew the likelihood of that happening was pretty slim, but if he was ever granted the opportunity, he would use nothing but the finest and best materials. He would take his time and think it through. Prior to the commencement of construction, he would spend years just developing his plans. Many nights after work would be spent sitting at his drafting table dreaming and drawing, erasing and walking through the hallways of his perfect Dream House. In his mind, he would float through each room . . . moving up and down, hovering and inspecting every detail. If it wasn't perfect in flow, function and beauty, it was erased . . . and drawn again.

Lawns and gardens, fountains, and gently flowing streams, fences and pastures and pastoral landscapes, surrounded by fruit trees and splendid views would all complement the outside. Inside his mansion, the rooms would be spacious and laid out in perfect flow with high vaulted ceilings and chamfered beams, edge-moldings and cornices. He had a special fondness for paneled woodwork and sculpted ceilings. His window jambs would be very deep so they could have large sills and angled sides with recessed beveled shutters posing as raised panels when not in use. Fireplaces would be everywhere. There would be no room in his Dream House where a warm fire couldn't be enjoyed.

When he wasn't performing his normal duties as a contractor and had a little time on his hands, he loved to dream and draw. He would settle for nothing but a perfect architectural masterpiece and he would work on it only when he wasn't in a hurry. His mansion would flow gracefully from room to room and fit to his taste like a tailor-made suit.

But he also knew that it would be only his Dream House on paper. He could never afford to build it. Now here he was, standing just a hundred yards away, staring at the exact design he would have built for himself, if money were no object and he had eternity to build it. Even the details on the outside were the very details he loved and drew. *How can this be?* he wondered.

Resting for a moment on a garden bench overlooking the estate, he allowed his mind to walk around the structure, caressing the architectural marvel before him. *Greek revival, my favorite*, he thought to himself. *Early Victorian era, with a Corinthian touch. So massive. Gorgeous, too! The huge columns, with those leafy accents at their tops, would make any apostle feel at home, and the second floor gallery would give honor to the most distinguished of Presidents. The owner must be very rich*, the man thought for a moment. *I wonder who lives here?*

Time passed without notice as he observed its beauty and contemplated its purpose . . . and his own. The man, though fully aware of its hypnotic attraction, didn't mind its beckoning tug. As if without choice, he succumbed to a curious and compelling urge that pulled him forward. He just didn't mind. He wasn't afraid of it. In fact, he wasn't afraid at all.

"I wonder who designed and built this?" he whispered to himself in a moment of professional distraction. He had to get a closer look, but he knew it would be presumptuous for a man covered with filth and dried slime to just walk up and knock on the door. His clothes were nothing but torn rags and his arms and exposed flesh were scarred and scabbed from bleeding. He was totally out of place and knew he was taking a huge risk, but something just kept drawing him onward.

He kind of knew what it was that was drawing him, but he was tired of analyzing his feelings. It wasn't about feelings anymore. He'd had them all in a single day and things were still what they were. In spite of the uncertainty, failure, doubt, fear, insignificance, terror, lostness, challenge, escape from certain death, aches and pains, torn clothes, and haggard appearance, one thing was sure. He was right here standing in this place. That was something he could comprehend. Another thing that he knew was that somehow, he was staring at the most beautiful work of architecture that he could have possibly dreamed of. That's all the psychoanalysis he could handle for the moment. All he knew was that he just wanted to touch it to see if it was real. Perhaps it was a hologram or he was on some strong medicine in a coma somewhere. For all he knew, Toto would come barking around the corner any second.

As he approached the front portico of the mansion and the ominous colonnade, the man felt a diminishing sense of importance, but it didn't matter. His inner curiosity simply pulled him onward with a divine expectation that none of this was by chance and feelings were getting old. He was tired of "feelings" ruling over him. So he reached his toe out like a little kid to touch the first step. When he felt it bump into his toe, he felt relieved. It wasn't a hologram in a sci-fi. Neither was he still in the jungle or delusional from fear. The step was real. He kicked it and it made noise. He felt a little bit like a curious deer, too; like he had just noticed something new in the woods that hadn't been there before. So he touched the step again. It was still there. The man looked to his right. Then he looked to his left. He looked behind him and he looked upward. He was curious, but he was nervous, too, just standing out there in the middle of the yard kicking the front step of the biggest mansion he had ever seen.

It was exhilarating! In this man's world of simplistic peasantry there were only small functional porches; not porches like this one. His porches were barely large enough to stand under to get out of the weather. For the most part, all he knew was simple posts, and affordable housing, and most of it was put together with biz-rate lumber, scrap, or anything he could get his low-budget hands on. Once in awhile, he got to build a beautiful house with a fair amount of detail, but he had never been commissioned to build anything like this. He wasn't even sure how he would write a contract for it.

The front portico entryway, with its massive double doors, fanlight, and sidelights, was now directly in front of him reflecting its own image through the mottled grains on the polished mosaic floor.

Some porch! he thought. *No bottom to the bucket here!* The man felt inches tall as he stood between the columns and glanced upward at the towering structure. He remembered how, as a child, his father would take him to visit Boston where he would look up the side of the Prudential Building and sense its movement against the sky. This was unlike any home he had ever visited, and he had seen some beautiful mansions in his lifetime. He had been to Newport, Rhode Island, and had toured many of them, there. He especially liked the pillars on the Marble

House, but this mansion dwarfed the Marble House. The Breakers was just over-built. It was too much, but the woodwork and craftsmanship was amazing and to think it was all done the hard way, not with routers and CNCs. He especially liked the gardens at the Rosecliff. He wasn't crazy about the mansion, itself. It was ok . . . for a camp. There was no question that all of them were man-made masterpieces, but he liked only certain things about each one.

In Germany, he had lived for several weeks in Bavarian Castles, and in Budapest he enjoyed beautiful evenings on the shores of the Danube and staying in Baroque Castles out in the country. In England, Austria, and Transylvania, he had marveled at the accomplishments of human ingenuity. Every one of those buildings were masterpieces of what man could accomplish. They were something to behold and although they boasted their own personalities, they just didn't feel personal like the one that was right in front of him.

This mansion was different. He liked everything about it. The columns, the second floor gallery with its airy expanse of antebellum ironwork and the overarching cornice combined to form a facade of heroic proportions, but something about it came down to his level and welcomed him. It felt like it just smiled, reached down, and shook his hand and said "Come on inside and rest awhile!" All those other mansions and castles that he had visited proclaimed, "I'm pretty and I can get really cold in the winter. So send me money! I need money! I must be maintained. It's going to cost a lot of money to keep me looking pretty!"

But not this mansion. Its front entryway, while obviously "Act one, scene one" of architectural expression, gave way to the mere height and breadth of this immense building. The portico windows, appearing proportionate from a distance, now stood huge as the man climbed the steps toward the door. Did I say "huge" again?

Its size, it's mystery, it's ominous silence, he thought. *I know I should be intimidated by it, but, for some strange reason, I'm not. I'm just not. Instead, I feel . . . expected . . . as if someone knew I was coming.*

As he put his hand on the door, he discovered that there was no lock on it. It glided open without making a sound, adding more mystery to the mystery. The exterior, though massive in appearance with its high style and royalty, now faded with each step into the polished interior, and finally relinquished itself as the door softly closed behind the man, with barely a click.

His mind, not able to comprehend inside and out simultaneously, submitted its perception to only what it could see. The foyer he was standing in, a true mezzanine, appeared larger in width than his entire house back home. There was a long hall with high ceilings and oversized doors placed symmetrically on each side. Their casings were uniquely applied around each opening with matching rosettes at the top corners. At the bottom, where the side trims met the floor, plinth blocks were installed to form a perfect transition with the layered base moldings. In the center and positioned toward the rear, a dual sweeping grand staircase, with multiple landings and balconies, reflected its craft and romantic swirl upon the high gloss of the polished marble floor below. The walls were decorated in pictorial wallpaper and accented with furnishings collected from early Victorian ordinance, leaving a stunning impression to the visitor's first glance.

As the man continued to explore the beautiful mansion, he was continually entertained with architectural and ancestral delights. On the first floor, room after room enticed him onward as if each one was trying to outdo the other . . . and he still had more floors to go. Everything the man looked at was exactly what he would wish for if allowed to build his own Dream House without worrying about the cost.

Suddenly, a previous thought occurred to him, only this time with obsessive power and resolve: *Who cares who lives here? Who built it and what's it doing out here in the middle of nowhere surrounded by that awful jungle?*

His attention began to focus on finding evidence or clues that could reveal the identity of the builder. He was Justa Carpenter, but he knew how to trace the work to the one who put it there. *Every builder leaves certain identifying marks*, he thought. *This should be easy.* He was feeling quite at home and relaxed. He was also feeling a little stronger and he was ready to do something productive, like figure out who built this place and find him.

So, with experience as his guide and with skillful application of his newly acquired detective skills, he began his search to find the builder. First, he would check the obvious places. Custom made cabinets and specialty woodwork always have the builder's trademark; but upon careful search, he couldn't find one. There was plenty of custom woodwork, too. It was everywhere; just like he would have done. But he was just getting started.

Undaunted, the next thing he would do was identify the hardware on the doors and windows and connect the manufacturer to the location and identify the builder who had purchased it. This would most certainly lead him to the builder. But again, there was no clue.

He continued his search throughout the mansion, but each time the man thought he was getting close, he came up empty. Now feeling a sense of mild desperation and challenge, the man was compelled to dig deeper. "I'll tear this place apart, piece by piece, if I have to," he sputtered in a kidding way. *Maybe if I trace the power supply, or the water source*, he thought to himself. *I'll get the name of the guy who owns this cottage and he can tell me who built it.*

As he followed the trail of wires to and from their destinations, he was astounded to find that even though there was plenty of electrical power, it seemed to come from nowhere! There was no evidence that any source of energy even entered the mansion, yet there was power and light everywhere! As if that weren't enough, the same thing was true of the water. There were pipes coming and going to their destinations, yet there was no outside connection to supply the mansion. But when he turned on a faucet, an endless supply of pure sweet water was available to satisfy any traveler's thirst . . . and satisfy his own he did.

"It's practically alive!" he said nervously under his breath. "I'm surprised I don't hear a heartbeat!"

He examined the heat source and discovered that, as with all the other utilities, the furnace operated without fuel yet provided an endless supply of warmth to his chilled and damp body. By now, the conflicting emotions of surprise and delight had exhausted his exhaustion. Whatever recovery of strength he had enjoyed was ebbing fast. As a builder, he had never experienced anything like this. He seriously doubted that anyone had. It was just here in the middle of nowhere! Certainly, nothing of this quality, precision, and magnitude could possibly just happen by itself.

"Oh, I suppose a member of the higher order of intelligence would come up with a theory about how it just happened. Before you knew it, his theory would be published. Then it would be put in textbooks and taught as fact and if you didn't agree, they would flunk you for disrespecting the theory."

It amused him as he pictured a professor demonstrating with professional looking charts how this mansion just fell out of the sky from a sudden explosion. Then he would wave his hands from behind his podium and demonstrate on his smart board how it all came together on the way down – concrete from China, excavated hole from an asteroid, heavy equipment from Caterpillar and John Deere, dump trucks from somewhere, cabinets, moldings, flooring, and tiled showers and all those electrical outlets from a whirlwind and . . . oh yeah, all the pretty landscaping. Then he would concoct a story on how it merged in perfect sequence, fell out of the sky and landed softly in its place between manicured lawns and gardens and walking paths and bridges and streams and . . . and all without any help from human hands or intelligent design," he muttered facetiously and then he stopped.

"No, actually they probably wouldn't do that with just a house, now that I think about it. Why do it with something as explainable as a house? That's limiting the mind in a finite way and we wouldn't want to limit the human mind in any way, would we? We should think bigger. Everyone knows that all houses are so simple to construct that we shouldn't even debate the notion that a house could fall out of the sky all assembled and ready to live in. They always like to defer to that billion year argument when they can't explain it scientifically. When that doesn't seem to work, they just add a second billion years or maybe a hundred billion years and assume that if something has enough time to happen, then it probably will. As far as they are concerned, the argument is over. Besides, how do you argue with the 100 billion year thing? Wouldn't it be nice if paint and roofing lasted that long?"

Such people never get it. Somehow, they have it all figured out in their minds even when the math, the science, nature, common sense, and even God, Himself, says otherwise.

But because he was Justa Carpenter, and his tiny mind being obviously handicapped by this, he could only know without a doubt that the jungle, the trees and sky, life and death, and yes, even this mansion that was right in front of him was planned and built by a master builder. He really wanted to find him and meet him. But, how would he find him and where would he begin looking if there weren't any clues? He would search his whole life for him if he had to. He must find him, somehow.

The man thought back to the confusion and futility of the jungle and his narrow escape from that "Thing." Then there was the discovery of the mansion. His first desire was to meet the owner, but that thought changed quickly and was replaced with an affection and admiration for the builder of this beautiful mansion. He would gladly give his remaining wealth and everything else that he had struggled for so long to hang on to, if he could just find him. Even the pursuit of wealth had become an insignificant concept, lost in another time and place. It didn't even belong here.

On the other side of the mansion, far across the lawn at the edge of the jungle, there were two stone pillars marking the entrance to the estate. From where he was standing, the man noticed that one of them had something written on it. It was a plaque with a name. He quickened his pace, believing that he had finally found his first clue. As he approached the closest pillar, he began to recognize a familiar pattern of letters engraved into a polished bronze plate. Then a cold sense of weakness fell to his hips and joints when he saw that the name on the stone was his own name!

Once again, he had to deal with conflicting emotions of delight and dread. But with no explanation nearby, he hated every moment and he didn't know if he could take one more heart-stopping surprise. For some reason, this beautiful mansion had his name on it, which could only mean one thing – it belonged to him.

But, how was it his? Was he . . . dead? Did that "monster thing" get him after all? Where was he, really? Other than birds, he hadn't seen a single sign of life; not a single person. Back home, wherever that was, all he wanted to do was get as far as he could from everyone. He just wanted to be left alone. Now he was desperate to find someone; anyone.

Where had he come from and how had he suddenly just arrived here, anyway? Part of him wanted to turn back and the other part of him wanted to stay forever. But, he knew he could never turn back. Each discovery only seemed to multiply his questions, yet no one could be found to answer even one of them. He couldn't imagine just taking up residence without knowing why it was his, or who had built it for him.

As he stood by one of the pillars near the edge of the jungle, he suddenly had a familiar sensation. There was no mistaking that feeling and he didn't like it. He knew it all too well. It was like the cold chill of imminent death. It was fearful and it weakened him. He knees just buckled and he was drained of strength.

Someone or some "thing" was near him again, and it

was watching him. He had allowed himself to get too close to the edge of the jungle and he knew it. He was afraid to look, but once again without choice, he cautiously turned around. As he did, he noticed a movement deep in the jungle. There! Again, a flash of white through the dense undergrowth. It was a person. He was moving, and it wasn't the man's imagination! He could really see him! He was near the bottom of the hill close to the edge of the bog; that awful bog the man had just escaped from. Someone, definitely a man, was looking right at him, but he was not like that other thing that had frightened him before. He wasn't hiding from him. In fact, he seemed to be intentionally revealing himself!

CHAPTER 5
THE BUILDER

T HE MAN FELT HOPE, AND A COMPELLING URGE to pursue him, convinced that he could answer all his questions. But he hesitated for a moment, remembering his close call with the jungle. He really didn't want to go diving right back into it. His skin had barely stopped bleeding, and he liked it right where he was. It felt safe. Why did he have to go back in there? He hated the jungle. He wished it would just go away.

But he knew that in order to pursue this man, he would have to break his previous vow and re-enter the jungle. So, before his senses could think it through and win, he took off and ran after him. His dreadful fear of that thing couldn't match his overwhelming desire to catch up to the stranger. This time, no "thing" would be allowed to get in his way and he was prepared to fight, if he had to, to get to the stranger.

So he left the safety of his estate and plunged back into the shadows and brush, weak knees and all, feeling the all-too-familiar grabbing and scratching of the thorns and briars on his already shredded trousers and torn skin. Undaunted, he continued his pursuit, relying on everything his heart and soul and mind and strength could give him. The stranger was only a hundred yards away now, and fresh glimpses gave the man hope and energized him with the remaining strength he needed to catch up.

Finally he got close enough to be heard. "Are you the builder?" the man shouted with a wheezing hoarseness as he leaned against a tree gasping for breath, "Or should I . . . should I look for someone else?"

He could see him clearly now. His spirit lifted and new strength came upon him when the stranger turned and waited for the man to catch up. As the man approached him, the stranger calmly spoke, "Yes, I built it," he replied. "Why do you ask?"

Catching his breath and almost not daring to ask the question, the man spoke with a sheepish voice.

"I need to know something, sir. The Mansion: Is . . . is it really mine?"

The builder responded by inviting the man to walk with him. He didn't seem to have even a slight fear or acknowledgement of the dangers in the jungle. In fact, he acted as though the jungle didn't even exist. He walked as if he were just walking down a street.

"Does it have your name on it?" the builder asked.

"Well yes, but. . . ."

The man suddenly forgot what he wanted to ask. His mind went totally blank. Feeling a mild state of panic setting in, and his composure about to crumble, he was glad when the builder spoke: "From where do you come?" he asked.

"I don't really know," the man replied nervously. "I just came through the jungle . . . barely . . . I guess. I was trying to get away from something. It was chasing me."

The builder looked at him, not speaking. He was just listening. He seemed to want to know how the man made it through the jungle. His eyes looked straight into the man's eyes, making him feel calm but a little bit uncomfortable, like he was waiting to hear him say the right thing.

"I, uh. . . ." the man stammered. "I never would have made it without staying close to those big trees and the vine and the roots. I nearly let go once. I . . . I'm really glad I didn't."

The man wasn't afraid of the builder for some reason, yet he hadn't expected to have to explain how he got here. Actually, he hadn't really given it much thought, until now.

"Roots," he remembered suddenly. "Those roots! If the roots hadn't been there to stand on, I don't know what I would have done. You know, the trees and the vine and the roots were a marvelous combination." He paused to catch some more breath. He was breathing really hard and couldn't speak more than a few words at a time. "I believed that I needed to depend on all three. I know one thing; my own instincts would've done me in, had I trusted them instead."

77

"Let's keep walking," the builder said to the man.

As he spoke he put his arm on the man's still quivering shoulder and led him out of the jungle and back to the estate. They walked quietly for a short while and the builder let the man calm down and relax. He was silent as the man slowly gathered his strength and composure.

Then the builder spoke, "I have something to say when you are ready. You must listen carefully to what I am about to tell you. Son, your prayer has been answered with a dream. But this dream is real and someday, you will be right here where we are standing."

He continued, "The mansion you have just seen is indeed your mansion. It's your eternal home in the future. It's my promise to you, and someday it will all be yours. It has been built with the kind of materials that you have not yet put on. Do you like it?"

The man was a bit confused. In his mind he wondered, *What materials? How do I send materials to build a mansion like this or put them on? What did he mean when he said "put on?" Where do you go to send materials for a mansion like this?* But he wasn't about to argue.

"It's everything that I ever would have dreamed of," the man replied. "But how can I afford to send materials for such a magnificent mansion and why is it so big?" he asked. "Don't get me wrong. I'm not complaining, I just don't feel like I deserve it."

"Well," the builder laughed, "like so many others, you dug a very big hole for yourself so I had to fill it with something!" But then he continued on, "You're right about the materials. They don't come cheap. One must be willing to pay the price or they just aren't available. You can't bring them with you, however. You have to send them on ahead. That's the only way they get here. There are no cheap substitutes in my mansions, no coupons, no discounts, no best buys, look-alikes, or liquidation sales."

He paused, then continued, "Years ago, when you came to my office. . . ."

"When? I mean, how did I come to your office?" the man interrupted. "I don't remember. I'm sure I wouldn't forget meeting someone like you or asking you to build such a place for me. . . ." Then, as though his mind was suddenly opened, he did remember. "The woods? That day all my problems began? That was your office?"

"The builder replied softly, "Everyone has a place that's special to them, and that's where we meet, but that's not my office. My office is here." He spoke, gently touching the man's heart. "When you asked me on that day to make your life count, no matter what it cost, you gave me permission to build, my way, and that's when the construction of your mansion began. You see, my mansions rest on a foundation of truth and promise. They are constructed by faith and obedience and a trust that I know what's best. Once the order is placed, your materials are manufactured and installed in many different ways. Actually, it's more like a 'putting on' than it is an installation."

"What kind of materials?" the man asked.

The builder paused for a moment and looked straight at the man. Then he replied with all the authority of a master builder, "I only build my mansions with materials that don't burn. During construction, I test the entire structure with fire to see what it's made of. That's not the only test, but it's the toughest one. If it passes this test, it really sparkles and we keep going. It more than sparkles," the builder said. "It shines."

"But, if it fails the test, then we clean up the mess and start over. The foundation remains intact."

The man thought for a moment and asked the builder another question, "What are the kinds of materials that would stand such a test?"

He needed to know.

"Through many trials and even more errors you will learn to recognize them all as you walk the walk," the builder replied. "But I'll tell you that even the most common of fireproof materials is put on with love. And not just any love. It has to be 'my first love.' Without it, nothing could survive the heat. This kind of love isn't cheap or easy to put on. It can only be acquired by persevering with long-suffering, and yes, sometimes pain and persecution and failure, loss, and the understanding of forgiveness . . . especially forgiveness.

These kinds of purchases require faith in my plan. When love is tested, it demands everything from you that you hold dear. Your investment would be worthless without commitment to these trials and tests. Shortcuts, quick fixes, cheap material, or cosmetic cover-ups won't survive the heat. After the test is complete, the final dressings of my mansions are crowned with the purity of brokenness and polished by the clean hands of a humble spirit. In between, as you know, there's a lot of hammering on raw material."

The builder continued, "Love not only changes you and prepares you for great accomplishments, love builds upon itself. Devote all diligence to this and a great mansion will begin to emerge from where a crater once was. As your mansion grows and you put on faith and virtue, true quality will begin to shine forth. You will also grow in true knowledge of God and will gain control over the lusts of your flesh because they just won't charm you like they used to.

Once the structure is fully tested, we can begin the final polish of Christlikeness. As you conform more and more to His image, you will also find it easier and easier to be kind to your brothers and love them with the same divine love that was shown to you; the kind of love that never runs out and whose fruitfulness finds its source of power from having been in the presence of the Lord, Himself."

The builder continued, "Through your present suffering you will learn to put on tender mercies, kindness, humility, meekness, and patience – all the things you asked for and knew you needed, but didn't have. These materials can really make a mansion sparkle. They not only build mansions, but they build great neighborhoods, too. You will learn to bear with one another, and forgive one another. Not only that, if anyone has a complaint against you or if you have a complaint against another; even as you've been forgiven, so also you will eagerly do. This is how you put on love and this is how construction is accomplished. Love is the bond of perfection where peace and thanksgiving really shines through."

The man reflected on his own troubles for a moment. "My own problems are designed to change me, aren't they?" he asked, like a child with a hundred questions.

"I shouldn't think of them as such a bad thing then, should I? But, what about my failures?"

He felt so foolish and ashamed of some of his failures. He had brought them upon himself and they were big ones.

The builder replied with a smile, "One of my favorite things to do is to take failures, weaknesses, and downright rebellious hearts and change them for good. You'll realize someday that I will cause all bad things to work together for good if you trust me and walk in my truth. That's a big 'if,' but when you do, you will think of your trials and failures as friends. Not only that, you'll let go of worrying about your past and will discover that your future is secure. I'm not worried about your past failures, so you shouldn't be either. I've got them covered."

"But . . ." the man started to say that some of those failures were pretty big ones, but the builder interrupted. "Sure," he said, "you have a bit of a mess to clean up back where you came from, but time isn't money here and we don't concern ourselves with deadlines, if you know what I mean. I prefer to build upward, not tear down. Even your mistakes can accomplish constructive change if you humble yourself and allow them to. You should see the kinds of materials that get delivered once a man begins to comprehend his position of blamelessness and experiences the changing power of grace. That's when love really begins to flow, and where love flows, mansions grow."

The man gazed at the builder's masterpiece, knowing full well that even though his mansion was perfect, he himself, was still far from it. But his mind had been opened to the power of grace. He knew that even if he tripped up and fell, he would not be hurled headlong because the Lord was there beside him, holding his hand. He might experience some damage to his joy and peace for a time, but he understood that there was a fountain and there was a stream to go to where he could be washed clean. It was on his own property and it was always flowing with pure water and perfect for washing and drinking.

Even if he went back and made a fool of himself again, he would simply confess his folly, return to what he ought to be doing, and press on toward the future. This is where he would rest his faith from now on . . . the promises of Christ. Until he arrived, he knew that there would be plenty more washings on the outside but now he understood that the inside has been cleaned once and for all. Only the outside would need an occasional bath; sometimes even a power wash.

The Prison of Unforgiveness and Bitterness

"But, how will I know when you are finished, if you don't mind my asking? Will I always have to endure such pain and humiliation?" the man asked.

"You tell me," the builder replied with a question. "You're a builder. What do you call a house when you are finished building it and move in?"

The man thought for a moment, then said, "I guess I'd call it . . . home."

"Well said," the builder replied. "And when every little detail of your mansion is finished, including the final cleaning, I'll call you home. That final cleaning is pretty intense and full of scrutiny. We give it the white glove treatment three times over. Then we clean it one more time after that. Nobody arrives here with one speck of dirt left on them from the world they came out of."

The builder continued, "I've always had this plan for you. In fact, the final design was hidden in your heart long before you even existed, but I only started building when you put your complete trust in me. When you put aside your plans, and accepted my plan, the unlimited resources of heaven were made available for construction.

"You know, I have a whole warehouse full of materials just waiting to be delivered. That's where you purchase such fine materials and learn how to put them on. In fact, it's the only place you can get them. Believe it or not, some of my clients won't claim them. For some reason, they insist on sending their own useless junk. Come, let me show you something else."

JUSTA CARPENTER

Chapter 6
The City

A S THEY WALKED AROUND THE CORNER TO THE PLACE where the entrance of his mansion met the jungle, the man's eyes were opened and he was astonished to see mansion after mansion. There was no more jungle. It was gone! All around him, as far as he could see, was a beautiful city with many mansions under construction. Some were complete and already occupied. Many were still in various stages of construction and some still had a long way to go. Some foundations had weeds and thorns growing in them and looked like they had been sitting a long time.

Some were just going into the ground. He could tell by the fresh dirt and the big holes. They weren't just holes in the ground either. They were craters! The man remembered his years of apathy, worldliness, and selfish pursuits and thought about his own foundation. He wondered how long he had caused it to sit there awaiting construction. It must have been a pretty big hole, too!

Free But Won't Come Out

On a nearby hillside, a once beautiful mansion looked as if it had been destroyed by a devastating windstorm. The remnants of "what used to be" were scattered all over the hillside leaving piles of debris everywhere. It made the man uncomfortable when he looked at it. Up until now, he'd thought that the mansions were indestructible. After all, didn't the builder build them?

"How could this happen?" he asked. "I thought your mansions were indestructible."

"They aren't my mansions. They belong to your brothers and sisters. In that case over there, the owner was unforgiving for awhile," the builder said, sadly. "He wouldn't love those who hurt him. He didn't want to pay the price for certain materials that were needed in order to guard against such disasters. He withheld them because they cost too much, and he insisted that we build on the foundation without them, instead. He said he would take his chances. He had to learn the very hard lesson that unforgiveness is like a prison cell. It is a dark and bitter place. He thought that his resentment and bitterness toward others was a way of punishing them, but he was only punishing himself."

"I can identify with that," the man replied. "Some time ago, disaster came upon me suddenly, and when those whom I thought to be friends blamed me for my own troubles, I became vindictive, even sought revenge. But that only added to my suffering and confusion and guilt and despair and discouragement. I felt alienated from everyone, including the architect. I even became alienated from myself, if such a thing is possible, because, try as I might, I lacked the power to make the doubts and fears and guilt and remorse and depression stop. They all just kept going round and round and round like a tornado, sucking the life out of me."

He paused, as the builder murmured, "And sucking the *love* out of you, as well."

The man nodded, remembering the darkness and his longing for death, and then he continued, "I even cursed the day of my birth," he said. "And I wondered if I had committed the unpardonable sin."

"I remember," the builder replied quietly. "Your brother, Job, cursed the day of his birth in his darkest moment. But he did not curse the architect, for something whispered that something good was going on; something he couldn't see."

"I heard that whisper, also," the man said.

"I know," the builder whispered. And when he did so, the man realized that this was the same voice he had heard when he had nearly lost all hope.

"It took longer than it should have to realize that the door of my cell was locked from the *inside*," the man said, "and that if I would only accept that everyone's sins, including my own, were already taken care of at the Cross, I could go free. Yet, even with the door already open, I still stayed in there for awhile."

"'Should have' is not relevant," the builder commented, "at least to us. Some stay in that place much longer than others, because the darkness of shame is more familiar, and the conviction that one should have to *do something to merit release* seems simpler and safer than just accepting the invitation to step out into the light of forgiveness. Those who remain the longest do so because their inflated sense of self-respect, which is really pride in disguise, insists there is something they must contribute to what has already been paid."

The builder looked again toward the city. "See all those mansions?" he gestured. "They all went through the same storm. It was a terrible storm, no doubt about it, yet they survived without any damage. That's because love is the perfect anchor that bonds each mansion to its foundation. Without the necessary anchor, a mansion merely sits unattached, relying on a false sense of security. It is vulnerable to high winds, earthquakes, and raging floods. Besides fire that tests for wood, hay, stubble, and anything else that burns, these are also necessary tests to confirm the presence of love. Nothing goes untested during the construction of these mansions. But don't worry. It's never final. They all get rebuilt, eventually. There are two reasons why," he explained.

"First, their foundations are solid and, second, I always finish what I start. Some owners have to learn to love and forgive the hard way, but they all learn eventually. It's a costly lesson, but eventually everyone learns how foolish they are to withhold love and forgiveness from others, or to reject forgiveness for themselves, thinking somehow their own case is unique," he said.

"Some are really stubborn and we have to rebuild multiple times. In some cases, we do it so many times that we

The Freedom of Receiving Grace

lose count. For some clients, it may be seven times. For some, seventy. And then there are those," he sighed, "for whom it is seventy times seven. I sighed not for us, but for them. My project manager has unlimited patience and he can wait out the most stubborn client. Eventually, when those clients see themselves for what they really are, they are ready to put on love and let us finish what we started."

He continued, "It's a beautiful thing to behold when they finally get it. But don't worry. There won't be any unfinished mansions in this city. Nobody is going to spend eternity living in an open cellar hole. When the city is completed there will be nothing left undone. No punch-lists or call backs. No vacant lots or burned out shells. If it were not so, I would have told you."

He paused, then added, "When the mansions under construction come crashing down in a storm or burn in a fire, we always rebuild them and when we do, they come out much stronger and better every time. Not only that, these experiences make our clients better at loving and forgiving because they have finally comprehended the fullness of unmerited grace and understood that the worst sin of all is their own pride and sense of self-righteousness, which must be replaced by humility and gratitude. Believe me, after investing so much for so long and seeing it all blown away or burned down, the client tends to want to do it right the next time."

Across another valley, the man noticed a few burned out shells and he thought about his own dreams and

The Hill of the Lord

goals and how they had all turned to ashes. He understood what a waste of time and effort it had been to invest in things that burn. If his mansion wasn't really complete, as the builder had said, he wondered just how far along it really was. He even wondered if his had burned or perhaps had blown away like the others. But as soon as that thought occurred, he realized that this was not for him to know.

But he did know one thing; after seeing the devastating damage that the storms had done to that other beautiful mansion, there was nothing anyone could do to him that he wouldn't forgive. That was the easy part. He had learned that forgiveness is not about forgetting. Forgiveness is remembering and still forgiving. Love emerges strong, not when forgiveness forgets but rather when love chooses no longer to remember. "Like the architect," he murmured, "who removes our sins as far as the east is from the west, and remembers them no more."

He knew, however, that his scars would remind him – those from the wounds of others and those from his own self-inflicted battles. Just because he had forgiven and found forgiveness, and just because the storms were calming down didn't mean the scars would go away. As long as he was alive, he would have those scars and he would have to choose how he would think about them when he looked at them.

The builder's hands were scarred, too, and the man knew that it was because of His scars that he stood there healed at that moment. In fact, the man knew that the builder's scars had been caused in part by his doing. The builder had every right to blame him for them. But he didn't. Instead, the builder's scars were reminders of healing and victory; something that never would have happened had the scars not been inflicted to begin with. Instead of remembering the injustice that was done to him, the builder just waved his scarred hands around and rejoiced over all the mansions that were getting built because of them.

The man knew that he must choose to view his own scars as friends. Learning to love would be a challenge, but he also knew that the power would be given him so he could do it. It was not going to be an overnight accomplishment. Learning to love would be a lifelong journey, but a good start would be to forgive everyone that he had held bitterness against. Then, should the painful memories return, he would remember the builder's scars and the blessing that had come from them.

He couldn't wait to imitate the builder and show forgiveness to everyone who had done him harm. But he wouldn't stop there. He would seek forgiveness from others for having done the same to them, knowing full well that he had no guarantee of receiving it. He recalled a verse about foundations in the Bible, which had challenged him in his spiritual walk, back when he had prospered financially: "Let them do good, that they be rich in good works, ready to give, willing to share, storing up for themselves a good foundation for the time to come, that they may lay hold on eternal life" (1 Timothy 6:18).

He wanted his mansion to be built on a good foundation; and he wanted it to be solidly connected. He knew that forgiving others was the purchase price for the bolts and anchors that would hold it securely in place during the next storm. He was not only willing to pay; he was anxious to do so. And with that change of heart, a vision came into his mind, of himself finally stepping out of that cell and into the light of life.

When this happened, the eyes of his heart were opened, and he suddenly understood the "adorning" of the mansion. It wasn't a structure at all. It was something that he put on. But before he could put anything "on," there was quite a list of things that he knew he had to put off. It was something he had to do; a purifying exercise of sorts. But there was more to it than just putting some things off and putting some other things on. The man knew that there were some things in his heart that he also needed to "put away."

It was an understanding that the builder had been waiting for the man to grasp, for it had been in their contract all along:

> "But now you yourselves are to put off all these: anger, wrath, malice, blasphemy, filthy language out of your mouth. Do not lie to one another, since you have put off the old man with his deeds, and have put on the new man who is renewed in knowledge according to the image of Him who created

> him.... Therefore, as the elect of God, holy
> and beloved, put on tender mercies, kind-
> ness, humility, meekness, longsuffering;
> bearing with one another, and forgiving one
> another, if anyone has a complaint against
> another; even as Christ forgave you, so you
> also must do. But above all these things put
> on love, which is the bond of perfection"
> (Colossians 3:8-10, 12-14).

> "When I was a child, I spoke as a child, I un-
> derstood as a child, I thought as a child; but
> when I became a man, I put away childish
> things" (1 Cor. 13:11)

> "Let all bitterness, wrath, anger, clamor, and
> evil speaking be put away from you, with all
> malice" (Eph. 4:31-32).

Below the mansions, a beautiful valley emerged from where the jungle used to be. All the mansions faced toward the end of it. On a hill at the other end of the valley, he could see others ascending a long series of steps to the top of a Holy Hill, silhouetted by its own brilliant light.

In silence he looked. In his heart he knew what he was seeing, and didn't need to ask any more questions about it. *Who may ascend?* he thought. *Only those with clean hands and a pure heart.*

His thoughts were interrupted as the builder spoke.

"Is there anything else?" he asked.

The man stammered in weak reply, "I, uh . . . can't think of anything."

The builder held him tight with his left arm. "Do you see the light now?" he asked.

Not knowing if he was standing on his own or being held, and sensing no adequate reply, the man remained in wise silence. He felt humbled and weak from losing his endless battles with fear and failure, not to mention his ugly pride which came at him in so many ways. He worried that he would never win that one. It would be a lifelong battle.

As a result of their dialogue, the man's past problems and failures had become a very far away and distant memory. His confusion had been replaced with an eternal promise of hope that nothing could ever take away. There was no darkness anywhere, not even a shadow that clouded his understanding. He now understood that all the painful trials and events in his life were loving touches of the master builder, who had always been in control and was simply building according to plan.

The man didn't want to ever leave but he knew he would have to do so . . . soon. Yet, somehow, that didn't matter. Wherever he was going, it couldn't be too far away. He knew he would be back someday and he looked forward to it. He was forgiven, and he would gladly forgive others and . . . accept God's grace for himself. Most of all, he realized the sustaining persuasive power of "loving first." He had seen it with his own eyes.

The builder continued, "You know, once I showed Justa Fisherman that I, not his fishing business, was his provider. He had been worried about how he would feed his family and pay his debtors if he followed me. One time he fished all night with nothing to show for it. He was exhausted. All his skill and effort had produced nothing, and he was very discouraged. But then I told him to cast his nets just one more time and he caught the biggest catch of his life. It wasn't about the fish. Once he understood that, he left his craft, his worries, and even all those fish and became a fisher of men. You're not a fisherman. But you both have the same first name!"

He paused, then added, "You are a lot like him. You think you are just an insignificant carpenter, but the reality is that you have a lot to offer to others, just like the fisherman did. From now on, you can be building men. When you return, you will be better equipped to strengthen and build up your brothers who are also struggling with the same questions and fears you have had. Don't be afraid anymore. You don't need to be anxious about your life. You can see that now, right? Put your trust in the master builder, and leave your cares with me. You needn't worry about anything, but rather commit your plans to me every day. I'll get it done. I promise; you won't be disappointed."

Again he paused, to let the thought sink in. "And oh, by the way, be a little easier on yourself while you're still human," he added. "You'll enjoy the construction a lot more. There's a fine line between self-examination and self-condemnation. There's a difference between accepting the responsibility you have to purify yourself and allowing me to do my sanctifying work of building you up. Many sincere clients who have since received their mansions never enjoyed the process because they kept worrying about everything they might do that would stop me or get in my way. Some were so serious that it could be said that they died of self-loathing. My perspective is that such concerns are not soul-threatening as much as they are joy-stealing. But really, who wants to be around someone who testifies about the joy, hope, and greatness of his salvation and then constantly whips himself over how bad he is in front of his friends who don't know me?"

He looked into the man's eyes. "Instead," he said, "you should awaken every morning and remember our contract. I have promised that I will complete what I have started. Before you even get out of bed, you should just rejoice that construction is underway! Then, when you are fully awakened, bow your head and entrust the day to the master builder, along with all your mistakes, trials, adversity, blessings, and victories."

Then he said, "Remind yourself every day of the promise that I am able to keep you from stumbling and look forward to the day when I will present you to the architect as perfect and complete and without blemish. Not only will I present you in perfect form and without fault, but I will do it with extreme joy! How's that for a contract? Wouldn't you rather live each day with this anticipation than in self-loathing and self-condemnation?

It's your choice, but either way you will receive your mansion when it's completed and either way I will still present you perfect and without blame."

The builder concluded with one more word of advice, "Do not worry – let me explain what I mean by that. Nobody gets a free ride and everyone must carry their own load. That's different from worrying. You cross the line into worry when you assume responsibilities and burdens that I never intended for you to carry. Your calling is to be faithful and full of faith. So be wholehearted in everything you do, as if you were right here working on your own mansion. The rest is easy, and because it's easy, you can rest. All you have to do is simply trust in my promises."

And he asked the man, "Do you think you can do that? For when you do, then you will have peace and freedom from worry. You'll also have a lot of new friends because you'll be a lot more fun to be around."

The man looked down at the ground, feeling a sense of unworthiness. With a deep sigh, he realized that he had been a proud man in many ways. Some of it was just sneaky, but it was still pride; the kind that expected more of himself than was ever there to give. It was the kind that threw fits when it made mistakes, saying things like, "I can't believe I did that!" Now he would entrust his mistakes to the builder, too, believing that he would cause good to come out of even his worst mistakes and he would stop thinking that he should somehow always be perfect in every way.

He would also stop complaining and grumbling when things didn't go as planned. Now he realized that all things always go as planned when God is choreographing the events of life. He realized that when God is working, then all things work "together." The bad things and the good things are all melded by God into perfect harmony for good. "If that is true, what is there to be complaining about?" he asked himself.

Letting go of his pride was one of the hardest tests he would face, for it was not just a form with many faces, it was a face with many forms. He realized that he had expected the finished product before it was complete and that, too, was prideful and impatient with the builder's timeline. He was relieved to know that he was under construction like everyone else who had put their faith in the builder. He was content to let the builder do what he did best, in his time, according to his plan, and in his way. He would try not to interfere by offering suggestions or by sending cheap substitutes or looking to take shortcuts; neither would he pretend to be more complete than he was.

He was done reminding himself of his failures in the past. He would leave his past where it belonged and entrust his future to the one who was so good at making bad things good. The man was calm and relaxed; completely at ease. For the first time in many years, perhaps ever, he was in perfect peace and without fear of the past or what stupid thing he might do today or what might even happen tomorrow.

As they stood overlooking the valley, the builder told him about the plan for the beautiful city. "Someday, when it's finished, we'll all be together; forever," he said. "No more pain, no death, no decay. No more failures, and . . . no weeping or gnashing of teeth!"

"When will that be?" the man asked, like the eight-year-old boy that he was when he had first met the builder.

"Only the architect knows when that will be," the builder replied. "He loves to draw! He is very patient and will wait until everyone receives a mansion who responds to his invitation to have him build one. But there will come a day when invitations cease and the great city will be finished."

The man asked the builder, "Will I ever get to meet the architect? He must live in an awesome home! Will I ever get to see it? The builder smiled and said, "You've been standing in it the whole time. Everything you see is His home."

The man was stunned. He felt undeserving of being included in the plans for the city. But he resolved to respond to the builder's love by giving back his own love in return. He knew full well that any attempt to match the builder's gift would be feeble by comparison, and he understood now that he never could have earned it. The cost to build a mansion like his was more than he could have ever paid. He could only receive it as a free gift. And receive it gladly, he did.

It had been a long day of fleeing from everything behind him and running as fast as he could run toward the only light he could see. Even so, as intense as that experience had been, it couldn't compare to the peace that came over him when he finally found the builder and saw him face to face. That changed everything. Most of all, it changed him. He would never again be the same man as the one who had emerged from the jungle. He didn't want to be.

"Respect" was hardly an adequate word to describe how the man felt toward the builder. It was so much more than that. "Awe" didn't capture it either, although there was plenty of that, too. It's not as if he didn't appreciate all the goodness, the generosity, the gifts and wonders that were all promised to him and it's not that he didn't appreciate his escape from that jungle "Thing," either.

They just all seemed distant considerations when he found himself in fellowship "face to face" with the builder. There was a new emotion as well, one that linked with the hope and forgiveness and mercy and grace that he had already received. It felt warm, like the lubrication of stiff joints that hadn't moved in years. It melted a cold glacial ice that had frozen over places in his heart that he had closed up several years before.

He really wasn't sure how to describe it because it was inexpressible. It was happening to him and he couldn't stop it. All he knew was that he felt whole and complete and lacking in nothing. Then he knew what it was. It was joy. It was joy, inexpressible. It was abundant joy. It was fullness of joy. It was "ineffable" joy, a word used to describe that which is indescribable.

He had read about this kind of joy in the Bible, but now he was experiencing it. He had always thought that such joy was reserved for those who lived better lives than he had. But now he was experiencing it in its fullness of fellowship. His joy was totally "full." There was no hunger for more, nor any inkling of less. He had joy, and he had joy inexpressible, and it was all because of the builder.

The Lord was his builder. What more could he possibly want? He didn't even think about wanting anything. Just the notion of "wanting" anything except to want to be with the builder seemed foreign and very far away from his desires. To want anything else besides being there with him would make as much sense as a starving deer craving more snow after a long, hard winter.

Yet he did, indeed, want something - to serve the builder. He wanted to please him. He wanted to bless him by bringing him pleasure. He regarded nothing the builder wanted from him as duty. He no longer saw his faithful service as an obligation. A command or a statute or a precept or a tithe? He loved them all! It was an honor to be his child. Nothing else mattered. He just wanted to serve the builder because he knew him. He had a personal relationship with him. He was his friend. He wasn't imagining it and he didn't make it up. The builder said it to him and he even put it in writing and gave it to him to keep by his side whenever he was tempted to doubt. He has been so wrong about thinking of him as a harsh taskmaster.

All he knew was that he didn't love the builder only for what he had done for him, although he had to quickly admit how much he did love what the builder had done for him. So how could he describe what he was feeling toward the builder? He just wasn't eloquent like some people he knew. He stumbled over his words most of the time. How could he explain to the builder that what meant the most to him was "HIM!"

He just loved "Him." It was a pure and undefiled love; a foreign concept in the world he was from. He had never known purity like this, either. How to love purely was hard to express when all his life his expressions of love always seemed tainted by some underlying self-serving motive that tagged along with it. But this time it was pure. For the first time, he realized that none of this was "about Christ." It "is" Christ. The ball and chains of bitterness and shame had fallen off and the coldness of his heart had thawed. He was free and he was free to love freely.

It had been a very long day, but the man was neither hungry nor tired. He had drunk all he could drink and his thirst was satisfied. Time had no relevance where he was. There was no darkness or night, not even a shadow; only perpetual light. He had a sense of total peace now as everything made sense, except one thing.

After a long pause, he spoke. "Sir? May I ask one more question?"

The builder nodded with a patient smile. He knew what was coming.

"What was that evil, terrible thing that was chasing me in the jungle? You must know what it was. It doesn't seem to be around anymore."

The builder put his nail-scarred hand around him one last time and with an affectionate tone, he replied, "My son, nothing was chasing you. It was just someone you needed to leave behind."

CHAPTER 7
A NEW BEGINNING

T HE MAN AWOKE TO A GENTLE BREEZE. It had dried the tears on his face, leaving salty remnants of the old life that he had left behind. He didn't know how long he had slept and he didn't remember the dream, but something within him had changed. There was a feeling of strength in his legs and knees that he hadn't felt in a long time. His head didn't ache any more, and his face felt relaxed. His neck felt loose and warm. For some reason he felt a strange security and a quiet inner peace as he got up and left that place a different man.

And when he had returned to his home, he sat down in a well-worn chair and opened his Bible for the first time in many years and read some of his favorite texts about the builder and how he worked. As he read, he could almost hear the builder's voice narrating, which made the passages come alive as they never had before.

And when he had finished reading, he prayed, a simple and short, almost child-like prayer:

Dear Lord,

If you are with me,
I have nothing to fear.
If you are against me,
I have nothing to live for.

Yours truly,
Justa Carpenter

And the Lord answered:

My son,

I will never leave you nor forsake you.
Be strong and courageous!
Do not tremble or be dismayed,
  for the Lord your God is with you
  *wherever you go."**

Sincerely,
The Lord your God!

P.S. If it were not so, I would have told you. †

*Joshua 1:9

✝

ADDENDUMS TO THE CONTRACT

THESE ARE THE PASSAGES HE READ, many of which he had underlined or highlighted through the years:

"The LORD has appeared of old to me, saying: 'Yes, I have loved you with an everlasting love; therefore with lovingkindness I have drawn you. Again I will build you, and you shall be rebuilt. . .'" (Jer. 31:3-4).

❧

"Let not your heart be troubled; you believe in God, believe also in Me. In My Father's house are many mansions; if it were not so, I would have told you. I go to prepare a

111

place for you. And if I go and prepare a place for you, I will come again and receive you to Myself; that where I am, there you may be also. And where I go you know, and the way you know." Thomas said to Him, "Lord, we do not know where You are going, and how can we know the way?" Jesus said to him, "I am the way, the truth, and the life. No one comes to the Father except through Me" (John 14:1-6).

"So now, brethren, I commend you to God and to the word of His grace, which is able to build you up and give you an inheritance among all those who are sanctified" (Acts 20:32).

"For we are God's fellow workers; you are God's field, you are God's building. According to the grace of God which was given to me, as a wise master builder I laid a foundation, and another is building upon it. But let each man be careful how he builds upon it. For no man can lay a foundation other than the one which is laid, which is Jesus Christ.

"Now if any man builds upon the foundation with gold, silver, precious stones, wood, hay, straw, each man's work will become evident; for the day will show it, because it is to be revealed with fire; and the fire itself will test the quality of each man's work.

"If any man's work which he has built upon it remains, he shall receive a reward. If any man's work is burned up, he shall suffer loss; but he himself shall be saved, yet so as through fire.

"Do you not know that you are a temple of God, and that the Spirit of God dwells in you?" (1 Corinthians 3:9-16).

<hr />

"For we know that if our earthly house, this tent, is destroyed, we have a building from God, a house not made with hands, eternal in the heavens. For in this we groan, earnestly desiring to be clothed with our habitation which is from heaven, if indeed, having been clothed, we shall not be found naked. For we who are in this tent groan, being burdened, not because we want to be unclothed, but further clothed, that mortality may be swallowed up by life. Now He who has prepared us for this very thing is God, who also has given us the Spirit as a guarantee" (2 Corinthians 5:1-5).

"Now, therefore, you are no longer strangers and foreigners, but fellow citizens with the saints and members of the household of God, having been built on the foundation of the apostles and prophets, Jesus Christ Himself being the chief cornerstone, in whom the whole building, being fitted together, grows into a holy temple in the Lord, in whom you also are being built together for a dwelling place of God in the Spirit" (Ephesians 2: 19-22).

"...being confident of this very thing, that He who has begun a good work in you will complete it until the day of Jesus Christ" (Philippians 1:6).

"By faith [Abraham] lived as an alien in the land of promise, as in a foreign land, dwelling in tents with Isaac and Jacob, fellow heirs of the same promise; for he was looking for the city which has foundations, whose architect and builder is God. . . . All these [heroes of faith] died in faith, without receiving the promises, but having seen them and having welcomed them from a distance, and having confessed that they were strangers and exiles on the earth. For those who say such things make it clear that they are seeking a country of their own. But . . . they desire a better country, that is, a heavenly one. Therefore God is not ashamed to be called their God; for He has prepared a city for them" (Hebrews 11:9-16).

"Blessed be the God and Father of our Lord Jesus Christ, who according to His abundant mercy has begotten us again to a living hope through the resurrection of Jesus Christ from the dead, to an inheritance incorruptible and undefiled and that does not fade away, reserved in heaven for you, who are kept by the power of God through faith for salvation ready to be revealed in the last time. In this you greatly rejoice, though now for a little while, if need be, you have been grieved by various trials, that the genuineness of your faith, being much more precious than gold that perishes, though it is tested by fire, may be found to praise, honor, and glory at the revelation of Jesus Christ, whom having not seen you love. Though now you do not see Him, yet believing, you rejoice with joy inexpressible and full of glory, receiving the end of your faith – the salvation of your souls" (1 Peter 1:3-9).

"To those who are called, sanctified by God the Father, and preserved in Jesus Christ: Mercy, peace, and love be multiplied to you. . . . But you, beloved, building yourselves up on your most holy faith, praying in the Holy Spirit, keep yourselves in the love of God, looking for the mercy of our Lord Jesus Christ unto eternal life. . . . Now to Him who is able to keep you from stumbling, and to present you faultless before the presence of His glory with exceeding joy. . . . " (Jude 1-2, 20-21, 24).

"Then I saw a new heaven and a new earth; for the first heaven and the first earth passed away, and there is no longer any sea. And I saw the holy city, new Jerusalem, coming down out of heaven from God, made ready as a bride adorned for her husband. And I heard a loud voice from the throne, saying, 'Behold, the tabernacle of God is among men, and He will dwell among them, and they shall be His people, and God Himself will be among them, and He will wipe away every tear from their eyes; and there will no longer be any death; there will no longer be any mourning, or crying, or pain; the first things have passed away'" (Revelation 21:1-4, NASB).

"There is a river whose streams shall make glad the city of God, the holy place of the tabernacle of the Most High. God is in the midst of her, she shall not be moved" (Psalm 46:4-5).

"And he showed me a pure river of water of life, clear as crystal, proceeding from the throne of God and of the Lamb. In the middle of its street, and on either side of the river, was the tree of life, which bore twelve fruits, each tree yielding its fruit every month. The leaves of the tree were for the healing of the nations. And there shall be no more curse, but the throne of God and of the Lamb shall be in it, and His servants shall serve Him. They shall see His face, and His name shall be on their foreheads. There shall be no night there: They need no lamp nor light of the sun, for the Lord God gives them light. And they shall reign forever and ever" (Revelation 22: 1-5).

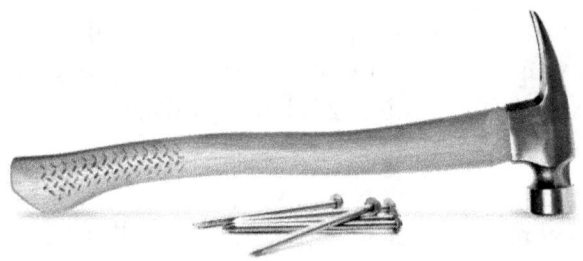

THEN, AFTER HE HAD FINISHED READING, HE WROTE THIS POEM, WHICH SEEMED TO SUMMARIZE IT ALL:

HIS PRESENCE - THE FLAME

There is a place to which I came in spirit to His Throne
With childish faith, not old or wise, just young I came alone
A "Friend of mine" I thought that day, would grant desires for
    which I pray
A miracle, promise, gift or two, His Love displayed must always
    prove.

My praise came shallow and camouflaged, expressed with pious
    greed
To serve the heart within me and fill its selfish need
My faith defined by what I get, a youngster still to learn
A lesson strong for all required, pass through His fire and burn.

This place I thought to which I came… His presence safe, secure
Where wing protects and shield rejects all tricks of evil's lure
My secret place of worship, knew only praise and peace,
A throne where love and mercy meet, and burdens sweet release.

But when came near His glory, was this time torn asunder
His Majesty unseen before, did sift my faith and plunder
Was not to me the place I knew, instead a place of terror
Where white hot fire consumed desire and light revealed my error.

His deepest probe, my inner thoughts where secrets well-concealed
In shadows lurk and comfort dwell are suddenly revealed
Where once I stood and felt so good, I soon began to search
Some place to hide my sinful pride and quench my selfish thirst.

His eye saw through chameleon's game, my compromise discovered
His holy stare, that awful glare, left not one thing uncovered

Justa Carpenter

I wonder now, what can I do, should I escape this flame
To stay through heat and torment, will IT consume my name?

Is not this the place where sinners come? Am I to be so bold?
To ask for sweet renewal; the promise I've been told?
Is not here the place He lends His grace? Why then, do I still bleed?
I do believe in you Lord. . . . Do you believe in me?

I, pulverized and broken, agree in desperate swear
To look within for hidden sin, to find its secret lair
Hurt deep and disillusioned, subdued with darkened hope
My empty soul repeats once more "Is this the God I know?"

I call His Name, my only hope, on promises I tread
Yet days go by, with no reply, just silence speaks instead
Will there ever be an answer? What child would He deny?
So dark this gate, my thirst so great, my spirit cries out "Why?"

Is an offering required of me? A vow I did not keep?
Can one who comes with empty hands make sacrifice complete?
Where's the key? Could ransom be? I'd pay whatever price.
"Conformed no longer to this world" ... Is that the sacrifice?

Jesus, God the Father, and Holy Spirit, Three
I came to you as One, but can offer only me
With emptied hands, broken heart, ashes, thirst, and gaunt
Transgressions beyond measure, I see nothing You could want.

Others seem so worthy, but I in fearful state
Believe the worst deserving, just kneel at Mercy's gate
Where low before the Maker, I bow in sin's disgrace
Confess my deepest longing, to feel the Lord's embrace.

While sinners mock my hunger, and suggest the drink of fools
My brothers spurn my longing, perplexed by solemn moods
With lips and voices singing, my wound they try to cover.
To drown their deepest fear.... The world is, too, their lover.

My thirst continues on - to know the Holy Son
No drink this world could offer, to match the "promised one"
Yet, inside a voice still screaming, Self's dominance still stands
"Give in and be replenished, forget the cross demand."

A battle rages inward, to escape this darkened school
Self aches to be replenished and drink old waters cool
A weakened man considers, for a moment, maybe two
God's silence, his own hunger, and the life that he once knew.

Waiting, waiting, waiting, I wait for His decree
Am left to my enduring, and drained of dignity
Life keeps its only promise, sure death its guarantee
Asks why God sees me dying, but shows no sympathy.

A crack of thunder rolls me under, His brutal Love replies
Compassion's flame attacks my name, and flesh begins to die
Darkness storms, His glory swarms, a mighty roaring blast
The Savior's glow, the Spirit's blow, God's presence moving past.

His Holy throne, His Royal home, where no approach can stand
His face so dread brings death instead but there I'm born again
A blast so fierce, so hot to pierce, it pulverized my soul
But soon the night, consumed by light, revealed my spirit whole.
Watching, He, with smiling face, unveiled His secret plan
One's death gives way to living, from death comes forth new man
Required the cost... submission, before one's hunger fed

He knows that we are ready, when we are finally dead.

They stood around my empty shell where my old nature dwelt
Old friends are stunned, they can't believe I chose His roaring swelt
"A Fool," they wag to one another. "Ignore sin's poison sorrows."
"Just laugh and drink the day away and party till tomorrow."

Even though my empty frame lies scarred from its own searching
The chaff and dross' removed by flame, and I'm no longer thirsting
Through dust and heat, dry wind and pain, His trail to holy cleansing
Emerged new life, new hope, new dreams, new songs, and a new
            heart dancing.

The place of His presence, where all must go
Where Truth reserves the final blow
For those who dare approach this throne
Will lose their life and die alone.

Ram's horn and trumpet's sound is clear
The flute and string fall silent here
No mind debates or lip shall speak
God's Word asks not... nor must agree.

A time will come when all must stand
Before the flame, God's wrathful hand
For those who choose to early die
God's hand of mercy purifies.
But some will choose cool shade and drink
Deny His flame consumes and shrinks
Life's pleasures beckon, they Truth despise
Will pay the price for trusting lies.

When in my youth perceived the cross
I sought its gain without the cost
My childish soul refused its price,
But I thank Him now, my sacrifice.
I thank Him now ... my sacrifice.

His Holy heat, a lesson sweet, white hot the burning flame
Would greet my prayer each time I dare in to His presence came
But I now invite His terror light to reveal my sinful shame
For quick I learned, each time I burned, removed eternal blame.

Sins Forgiven, Sin forgotten,
Life reborn, life begotten
Salvation's gift, from dying seed,
New birth in Jesus, this my creed.

I wrestled the Savior and passed through His flame
I entered His presence and lost my old name
Not a kid anymore, His plan is now plain,
Not my way but His, my dying ... my gain.

High above, in God's white hot love, where sins need not defend
Am seen by Him as clean within, but I know I can't pretend
Though changed am I, the price was high, and ugly scars remain.
But rejoice with me for though I walk with a limp ...
I walk with a brand new Name! †

www.ingramcontent.com/pod-product-compliance
Lightning Source LLC
Chambersburg PA
CBHW072357190626
46811CB00019B/1212